Jungle Truth

In the thickest part of the South American rain forest, the temperature is always as high as the humidity. A body could break a sweat just sitting in the shade. The flighty, colorful birds here are louder than some automobiles back in America.
This is the place two scientists, Doctors Jonathan Breech and Michael Dunaway, are currently calling home away from home. They are in their third month of a two-year research on rare to extinct plants in this region of the world. The West Virginia laboratory they work for received second-hand information that some flowers thought to be extinct for more than 2,500 years, still grew in this place. After four and a half weeks, the lab got all the necessary funding and chose their team to run the expedition. They went through only a few applicants before teaming up Breech and Dunaway, again. This duo for hire had had positive results on their last two expeditions.

Dr. Jonathan Breech is a thirty-eight year-old American scientist. He graduated Boston College at the young age of twenty-three carrying with him two Masters and two Bachelor's degrees. He has been playing with bugs, rocks, and plants since he was a little boy growing up in the Southwest next to a Native American reservation. His mother is a medical technician and his father is a doctor. They frequented the reservation where they were always welcome to do free physicals and lab work. The casino money made on the reservation built their office/lab. While his parents worked, the natives taught young John the ways of desert life. His boyhood interests consisted of the plants, animals, insects, rocks, and even wind and water movement within this environment. By the time he was twelve, he knew almost every plant, rock, flying, prowling, crawling creature, in the desert. He could not read enough about them. As he grew, so did his interests.

He graduated high school at the early age of fifteen and was accepted to Boston College with open arms. The books he gained access to there were phenomenal. Furthermore, with the help of their computers, he was able to travel the world without ever leaving the classroom. After graduating college, he did not go to work for one company as he had planned. Instead, his interests guided him to freelance research working for different colleges, laboratories, and high-tech, all-natural medicine and cosmetic companies.

During his seventh year of research he was given a short assignment in Peru. It was there he met a slightly older man named Michael Dunaway, a native-born Australian. Dunaway, unlike his younger colleague, did not receive his knowledge from the classroom. He read all the time. Both, however, got to study with legends of the world. Breech learned from the Native Americans and Dunaway learned from the Aborigines. Michael grew up in the outback and was tutored from home. His mother and father were both park rangers who oversaw more than 4,700 acres of rugged Aussie wilderness. What schools and books didn't teach this family, the natives did. Young Michael had teachers growing up; they just didn't live in boxes.

Dr. Dunaway's first impression of the younger Dr. Breech was not what he had expected. Rather than a snot-nosed Boston graduate, he was eager to learn from anyone who knew about the great outdoors.

They worked well together with very little conflict. Peru was the first of many assignments they would enjoy together.

Their current South American expedition has been one of slow interest. The clan of people they were working with were very knowledgeable about every living thing in the jungle. Since these people were well known in this region, the doctors took a crash-course in their native language. Fortunately for both, one of the natives, Anuk, spoke fluent English.

Years ago, the elders had ordered Anuk to go into the "large crowded villages" and learn this language from the English speaking people who would come trapsing through their jungle home.

Anuk worked as their mediator and guide. Though he was not an elder, he was given almost the same respect as one by the tribe, of about twenty-six. His father, however, was an elder. Anuk taught the younger boys coming of age, about nine or ten years old, how to hunt, track and fish. He also taught which animals, plants and insects were edible and which were dangerous. He even taught them some English, by request of the elders. Since the two scientists joined their campfire, a sign of welcome to visitors, Anuk has been assisting them with such things as plant and animal life locations, tribal dialect, and ceremonies and traditions. Rule number one: Do Not Disrespect the Elders, rule number two: . . .well, that is the only real rule.

The eldest son has been a tremendous help to the western doctors. His age, possibly late forties, was not really known because these people did not celebrate birthdays, keep time, or use calendars. Every day is life without looking back . . . 'When hungry eat, when tired sleep.'

The American team had been with the Utau tribe for almost three and a half months before things really got interesting. Their hopes of finding rare plant-life would soon exceed their expectations. The nights found them gathered around a campfire with the elders' stories traveling across a warm breeze. This night has turned to one great interest for the two curious scientists.

While sitting around the small comfortable fire, the scientist overheard a strange word not heard before.
"Anuk?" Dr. Breech asked. "What is that word the elders speak of?" Several faces stared blankly at the scientist. Anuk translated to the elders what the doctor had asked. The campfire area got ghostly quiet. One, two, three, four at a time started walking away from the fire.

~ III ~

By the time everyone had walked quietly to their huts, the four elders, Anuk, his predecessor Ranu, and the two scientists were all that remained by the quiet crackling fireside.

"Well," remarked Breech, "It looks like I've struck a nerve."

"Or two nerves." Dunaway said with jaws opened as wide as his eyes. "You sure know how to clear a room mate."

"Anuk?" The bewildered American began to ask. "Did I say something wrong?"

"The place we speak of has no name. It is forbidden for anyone to go there. Only elders are allowed to speak of it."

"Why? What's there?" Breech pushed further. Anuk looked at the elders, spoke a few words, got a nod of approval, and then began to speak to the scientists, now on the edge of their seats.

"This place we know of is what we call 'badgood.' It is a place of much mystery."

"What kind of mystery, mate?"

"The plants are strange there, one day dead, the next day alive."

The scientists turned slowly and stared at each other.

"Anuk," Breech started as Dunaway was nodding his head in agreement to an unasked question. "Can we see this place, this . . . mystery?"

Anuk turned to the elders as a small discussion took place. After an eternity of thirty seconds, Anuk turned around to speak to the nosey Americans.

"The elders say you have helped them and the tribe to better understand how jungle life grows and to obtain medicines from plants. They say you might help them understand the mystery place a little better with your science. They have discussed this before because of your curious nature."

"You mean we can go?" Breech asked.

"Next full moon," Anuk stated.

"Why the full moon, mate?"

Anuk stared into Dunaway's eyes. "It is the only time I know its location."

"What in blue blazes are you talking about?" questioned Breech.

~ IV ~

"It is never in the same place. It moves."

The elders started walking to their places of rest.

"Gardens and forests can't just bloody walk off."

"You will see what I mean next full moon. Good night."

As Anuk smiled and walked to his family's hut, the two were left to themselves talking in the night by a dying fire.

"What the bloody hell is 'blue blazes'?"

Breech's laughter ended the night.

Needless to say, the days that followed were filled with more questions than answers.

When the day arrived, they began by packing for their next day's journey. Anuk told them the journey would take about two and a half days. Both, on a five day in and out trip, would usually pack seven days of rations for emergency. However, with Anuk as their guide, they would be able to eat anytime along the way; a few days' rations would do. He was able to cook up a large variety of jungle food, but you somehow cannot get away from the flavor of dehydrated potatoes and corn. After all, iguana cooked so many ways is still iguana.

The next morning, the three were given a small blessing ceremony before they voyaged off. About twenty minutes later, they were on their way. Goodbyes were said as Anuk led the three toward the southwest vicinity. They walked for about five hundred meters before conversation broke out. One after another the scientists asked Anuk question after question. After a short preview of what the rest of the trip was going to be like, Anuk halted the questions with, "You damn Yanks will have to see for yourself!" Both scientists laughed until their sides hurt. Anuk had never cursed before, at least not in English.

As echoes of laughter rolled through the valleys, the three pressed on until that evening camp-break.

"Anuk," Dunaway started as everyone was unrolling sleeping gear, bathing and cooking supplies, "If no one is allowed there, then how come you know about the place?"

"I found it in the afternoon of a full moon when I was a young boy. The next day I go to look for it, it was gone."

"Gone?!" Both Westerners gasped loudly.

"Yes, or I could not find its location."

"Then you could've just gotten lost." Breech spoke with concern.

"I went back several times during a full moon. It will be in a certain valley at that time. We will have only twenty-four hours to find it and leave."

"How can a bloody part of the jungle just disappear?"

Anuk chuckled lightly. "You are the bloody scientists. You tell me." Breech let out a laugh as they started their night fire.

Morning came with birds of all colors, shapes, and sizes whistling to the rising of the warm sun. Though still under a dark canopy of colossal trees, night and day were still very different. With the fire crackling, the two scientists woke just as Anuk was walking back into camp carrying two fish. Breakfast was cleaned, cooked, and consumed in an hour. After clean-up, packing, and coffee, the three were on their way.

After a five-hour walk, they cleared the vegetation that served as their earthly blind to the universal space. Finding specimens all along the trip, they dared not load up on weight before coming back. Anuk assured them that they would be traveling this exact path back.

"You see the two trees that grow as one," Anuk said, pointing to his right side on a hill, "you will see it again."

On a hill under bright sunlight, two different types of trees grew as one. They were approximately 20 feet high and six feet wide at the base. They were intertwined at the roots to about twelve feet off the ground, and then separated into two different trees. One was bearing fruit and the other flowers.

"Remarkable," said Breech. "The science world would love this."

"Yeah, mate. They'd love to chop it down and carry it back to a lab."

Both Breech and Dunaway had a grim view of the way some people in the science field treated 'life'. After all, some of the finest mystics in the world taught them respect for nature.

After a few more hours of walking through valleys of large trees, but not thick jungle, Anuk started leading his curious companions up over the ridge of a very large hill. When they rounded the other side, he stopped and waited for his team to catch up. First Breech, then moments later Dunaway got to the top where Anuk was waiting.

"My God, how beautiful," Breech whispered as he stared into the largest valley of trees he had ever seen, trying to catch his breath.

"You said it, mate." Dunaway wholeheartedly agreed.

"We will camp there," said Anuk, pointing to the right of the valley. "We will reach our destination tomorrow before noon." As they trekked counter-clockwise down the small ridge of the southeast side of the valley cliffs, they noticed an overgrown path. "Anuk, this path was used at some time, wasn't it?"

"Yes. My people used to live in and out of this valley for many years. There used to be thousands of us before the diseases of the light-skinned hunters and treasure-seekers. Now only three or four hundred are left. We have scattered ourselves into small villages so we cannot die out all at once."

Their footsteps echoed over a short 5-minute silence.

"Anuk?" Dunaway broke that very silence. "Your people allowed us into your village. Why?"

"You are a scientist. Scientists and doctors healed many of my people when some outsiders found out that the Western, common cold was killing thousands of people. They are considered medicine men and deserve much respect. About sixty years ago, when disease was killing my people . . ." Anuk paused to remove a small log from across the path, "my people thought the garden was punishing them for befriending the light people. They moved out of the valley, never to return. Soon after, doctors and scientists came in with many medicines and helped my people.

~ VII ~

After returning from school, I taught my people the ways of the light people. I showed them that they do what they do because they are ignorant, not evil."

Breech and Dunaway stopped clearing a few small vines in their path and stared at each other with a 'what can you say' look on their faces. Then, they continued on as Anuk kept speaking. "Then my people just let well enough alone and left the garden and valley in peace."

"Anuk, mate, your English is sometimes better than mine."

"I had Western teachers in school and graduated with honors."

"Look out, Dunaway," Breech commented, "You're not dealing with a spring chicken here."

All three chuckled as they chopped, and climbed their way down the vine covered rock path. As they reached the bottom, the rock path turned to earth and forest. With very little undergrowth, they moved a lot faster.

After two hours of forest trekking, they broke camp with a cool comfortable breeze at their back. They could hear a waterfall in the distance.

"Showers tonight, eh mates?" Dunaway smiled while unpacking.

After camp was set, the three headed off to the showers. They walked west about 150 meters and came to a crystal-clear swimming hole at the base of an eight-foot wide waterfall. The ten foot wide stream wound southwesterly toward the direction the three would be traveling at sunrise. "Last one in is a rotten egg!" Breech yelled loudly then took off running.

"No, you don't!" Dunaway was hot on his heels.

"Wait!" yelled Anuk. Both men stopped dead in their tracks. What danger did he forget to tell them? Anuk rushed to the water's edge and stopped, and then looked his two comrades very seriously in their eyes. He stuck his toe in the water, grinned and jumped in yelling; "Now you both are rotten eggs!" The two geniuses had been had, and jumped in laughing.

On the way back to camp, Anuk told them more stories of his people living in the valley.

~ VIII ~

"The garden would never appear in or close to the village. According to my father, he remembers it being about two hundred meters away one time. The elders seemed to agree with him. They have many stories."

"Anuk," Breech interrupted, "how many times did you go there as a child?"

Laughing lightly, he replied, "Too many times."

"But, I thought the place was forbidden."

"Not as much as we would like the children to believe. There could be much danger there."

After returning to camp, the professors got ready for chow while Anuk took his spear and headed toward the stream. About a half hour later, he returned carrying a large fifteen-pound solid black bass on his spear.

"That didn't take you long, mate. Grimy, look at the size of that fish!"

"What in blue blazes is it? It looks like a largemouth bass . . . but the blamed thing's solid black."

Both men walked over to investigate just as Anuk threw their unusual dinner across a log.

"Look at the size of his eyes."

"Yes, they're the size of half dollars."

"Anuk, did this come from the stream we were in?"

"Yes, about fifty meters upstream."

"I just found my new fishing hole." Dunaway replied.

"Michael, old chum, the lab is going to be more than enthusiastic to see what we've found. Anuk, you're gonna make us famous."

The three chuckled as dinner was prepared. With the jungle spices in hand, Anuk cooked the fish as fine as any Boston restaurant. The two scientists used different ground roots, flowers, and fruits to make up some of the finest cooking spices to encounter the human tongue. With Anuk with them, they could eat like kings in the jungles of the world.

~ IX ~

The next morning was received with much anticipation. Not able to sleep much the night before, the team got ready to break camp early, after having leftover, seasoned black bass with morning coffee. With about an hour's sleep between them, they talked aloud about what the garden site would be like, like children the night before Christmas.

"Oh, by the way Breech, where's Anuk?"

"Oh yeah, he said he'd be back shortly. There was something he wanted to bring us."

"Bloody hell, he's gonna bring back a two-headed toad or something." Dunaway chuckled.

"No, I think this is more the soulless type. Some fruit or berry or somethi...speak of the devil."

Anuk walked into camp smiling, carrying one of their small tote bags.

"What 'cha got, mate? Nothing with a heartbeat, I hope. I got no place to put it, yet."

"No, come and see." Opening the tote bag, he revealed dozens of what appeared to be small green coffee beans that reeked of sassafras.

"Whooo. Would you smell that?"

"Smells like it would make some bloody good coffee."

"Anuk, is this edible?"

"Yes, very bitter, very strong."

"Good. We'll have green coffee in the morning, then."

"You will need it."

"Why?" asked Breech. "What do you mean?"

Anuk smiled and said, "Time is different there. Not harmful, just . . . you will see."

After a final light repacking, the three headed west toward the swimming hole, and then southwest along the clear stream. After an hour and a half of walking, the stream took a turn to the southeast.

Anuk turned and said, "This is where we cross."

~ X ~

The three took turns swinging on one of the vines across the narrow stream.

"Hey, look mate. I'm Tarzan!" Dunaway laughed as he crossed to the other side.

Anuk commented, "We are almost at the site."

"What should we look for, Anuk?"

"Flowers or thorns."

"What?"

"The site will be impassable due to thorns, or surrounded by flowers."

"Impassable? What do you mean, impassable? You mean there's a chance we can't get to it?" Breech was getting excited.

"Not quite," Anuk replied, smiling. "To the east there is an opening, as if the thorns cannot grow there. It is about thirty meters wide. The rest is impassable, except for the opening."

"Let's just get there. I'm getting blue blazes just thinking about the place."

Breech laughed. "You've almost got it, mate." He picked at his Aussie friend as they moved on. About an hour later Anuk stopped. "It will be within 600 meters from this point," pointing in front of them.

"You don't know its exact location?"

"No one does. But it will be there." Anuk smiled as the three moved on with piercing anxiety. "We will have plenty of time. Trust me." Anuk appeared very confident. Staying within ten arm's lengths of each other, the herbal treasure-seekers moved wide-eyed through the beautiful forest.

After about an hour and fifteen minutes into their search, Dunaway yelled, "Hey! Quick, I think I found something!"
As the other two were rushing to his location, he moaned aloud, "Sorry, mate."

Breech sighed in disappointment as he had just reached his partner.

~ XI ~

"It's just a large stone covered in flowers. No flower wall, or thorn wall . . ." Dunaway's voice faded in a near miss.

"That's alright," Breech moaned in disappointment as he turned to walk back to his original search path. Just as Breech was turning around, Anuk reached Dunaway's position.

"False alarm, mate. It's only a rock of . . ."

"No! You found it! You found one of the pillar gates!" Anuk said with excitement.

"What?"

"Look!" Walking around the huge ten feet high and ten feet wide rock, Anuk was feeling with his hands under the white-flowered vines. Reaching the other side of the rock, he yelled excitedly, "You see? This is it!" Pulling back the white and green veil, he revealed an image engraved in the side of the stone, a little worn by weather but highly detailed.

"What in the bloody blue blazes . . .?"

"Now you've got it, mate. It almost looks like an eagle with no wings. Look at the detail of his robes. Dunaway, our friend Anuk here has just shown us an archeological discovery."

"It's spectacular, mate. But where's the bloody garden?"

"Right behind you," Anuk whispered as he was facing southwest of the stone figure. The two scientists turned at the exact same time and stared in awe at the most beautiful place they had ever seen. It was a valley where the trees were different heights and loaded with many kinds of fruits and all different types of flowers as far as their eyes could see.

The three stood silently for several minutes. A colorful low flying parrot snapped them out of their trance. They looked at each other smiling as if they had just won the lottery.

"We couldn't see it till we were right up on it. I'm not eeeven gonna ask how. Let's get our equipment," Breech said.

"I'm ahead of ya, mate."

"I will carry something." Anuk followed the two around the other side of the statue to retrieve the gear.

~ XII ~

In less than three minutes, they were walking through the garden's "gate". The garden appeared to be about 250 acres in size. The trees there were spectacular. Every fruit and vegetable plant on earth seemed to be in this one particular part of the jungle.

"Look Breech, a nine-foot coconut tree!"

"That's nothing. Look at this fresh okra the size of my wrists." The two scientists heard some tree rustling and looked up to see Anuk shimmying up a fifteen-foot banana tree.

"My God," whispered Breech as he glimpsed Anuk's prize at the top. "I can't believe it. Those bananas must be two feet long, and as ripe as you could hope for." The three men were like kids in a candy store. After an hour of giddy, jungle, grocery shopping, they all gathered together to examine their finds.

"Look at all this, Breech. It's fantastic."

"No one back home is gonna believe this."

"No," Anuk interrupted. "No one can know of this place. It is very sacred. Many people will come . . ." Dunaway put up his hands to stop him. "We know, what too many people can do to an environment."

"Yeah," agreed Breech. "We won't tell a Soul."

"The mission never spoke of, huh, mate?"

Breech smiled and nodded. The three shook in a pact.

"Well," said Dunaway, "let's see what else we can find." Leaving their finds stockpiled on top of the velvet green grass, they moved westward. There was so much to see and examine, they had to limit one specimen per plant type. Of course, a two-foot long banana unpeeled weighs up to 2 pounds.

Their weight was limited since they would have to travel two and a half days back, or so they thought.

"Hey, Breech." Dunaway stopped moving. "Ya feel that?"

"Feel what? I don't feel anything."

"Yeah, mate, that's what I mean. No stinging, pinching, biting, annoying insects."

~ XIII ~

Breech stopped like a statue. "You know. .you're right. Those little pests haven't harassed me since we walked into this paradise. You don't think there's some sort of natural repellant put off by all these flowers, do you?"

"Frankly mate, I think the place is just too perfect for them to exist."

"Well, I'm not complaining old man."

Breech grinned from ear to ear.

Moving at a curious pace, the three found wonders no other white man had ever seen, or ever will. Grapes the size of silver dollars, and cantaloupes the size of bowling balls were just some of the wonders that crossed their glorious path.

After about thirty minutes of paradise shopping, they stopped at the northwest part of the garden. The entire corner of the garden was cut off by a beautiful, two-foot wide, semi-rocky stream that created its own seclusion. There were no bushes, plants, or trees of any kind growing there, except one. Plush green grass, that looked like it had been kept up by a very expensive gardener, covered the entire area. The three-foot wide tree was about twelve feet high with fruit branches that hung down to about five feet off the ground. The tree was loaded with the shiniest fruit you could ever imagine. They glistened as if they were wax polished, every single one.

"They almost look like blue pears," Breech quietly said in amazement.

"Bloody hell," Dunaway started. "That tree looks to be a thousand years old." The three walked over to the edge of the narrow stream.

"Yeah," Breech said. "It does look ancient."

"This is what the elders say is badgood. It is both cursed and blessed."

"Anuk? How can it be bad and good?"

"It is both dead and alive."

"Well it looks very much alive to me, mate. Look at the brilliant shine on that fruit."

~ XIV ~

"Yes," smiled Anuk. "You will see soon."

"I'll bet you don't have blue pears down under," Breech said as he was walking around their new discovery.

"I'll bet the bloody things aren't in America, either."

"Well," Breech started, "let's pick a couple and get a soil, leaf, and bark sample and we can head back through the other part of the garden."

"Agreed." Dunaway nodded. "Anuk? Anuk?" The scientists, in their own state of curiosity, had not noticed that Anuk had not approached the tree with them. He was still standing close to the water's edge, about twenty feet away.

"What's the problem, mate?" Dunaway asked on his knees as both scientists stared at him.

"This tree is sacred to many people. I am not an elder. I am not allowed to touch it. I did as a child . . . but I was just a child."

"Respect for elders and tradition, I like that," smiled Dunaway as he finished his soil sample. After all their samples were taken, two of the pears of fruit were wrapped up and then everything else was packed.

"Anuk," Dunaway said as he was throwing on the backpack carrying the sacred site's vintage. "I'll tote this pack myself, mate."

"Thank you," Anuk smiled as he stepped back across the two foot wide stream. Taking a right, they walked about thirty meters before turning left back to the eastern gate. They had walked about five more meters when Dunaway blurted out, "Bloody hell, look at this." Growing a few feet to his left, was one of the most beautiful white flowers imaginable.

"My God, it's breathtaking."

"What is it?"

"It's a Penta."

"I've never heard of it." Breech commented.

"Not many people have in the States. This rare beaut' is almost 2,000 years extinct in Australia. This is a very rare find."

~ XV ~

"I wonder what it's doing growing here." Dunaway replied.

"You gonna transplant?"

"No, mate. I could never tell anyone where I got it."

"Yeah, I kn . . ."

"Oh, a Penta," Anuk said as he peeped around Breech's left shoulder.

"A what?" Both men asked at once.

"It is a Penta."

"You know this flower, mate?"

"Yes. Northeast of village, they grow in cliffs near waterfall."

"Bloody me. This'll make us famous in Australia, mates."

"As if we don't already have work to do." Breech interrupted with a grin on his face.

The three moved on. Every twenty steps there was something to behold. One of many items that they stopped for was a bright red honeysuckle the size of an Iris bloom.

"Breech, look at the size and color of those suckles."

"Whew!" gasped Breech. "I could smell those twenty feet away downwind.

You smell that?" Breech nudged Anuk, as he stood with his nose in the breeze.

"Hey Dunaway!"

"Yeah."

"You smell that?"

"Mate, I think I smell fresh strawberries . . . big as beach balls, no doubt."

He grinned openly. After carefully collecting one of the honeysuckles, they moved on.

"We'll be eating good tonight, huh Anuk?"

"Yes, very good." They smiled as they walked.

After another twenty to thirty feet, the smell of strawberries filled the air in this particular spot in the garden. Then, on the ground running alongside a three-foot row of miniature peach trees, the huge leafed strawberry vines grew.

And on those vines were no doubt, the largest, ripest strawberries on planet Earth. They were as big as your fists.

"Jackpot, mate." Dunaway, in the right position, was the first to spot their bright red treasure.

"A couple of those will do nicely," Breech commented as he approached the small thick patch. "They never sold berries like this in Boston."

"We'll 'ave too much to carry out if we're not careful, mates."

"I agree. One or two more and we'll have our fill."

"We could cut across to the banana tree there," pointing in towards the north, "and pack up what we've left behind."

"Yeah, we should find a couple a' more tasty specimens between heyre and theyre."

"Dunaway," Breech started laughing slightly, "Your Aussie accent is getting heavy, real heavy."

"Yeah, mate. It happens when I get excited, and I've been excited since we walked into this place."

"Yes, exactly." Breech's eyes lit up. "Look at us. We haven't stopped smiling since we walked into this edible paradise."

"Yes," Anuk said. "My face hurts."

The three laughed as they walked. After reaching their ready-picked groceries, they packed up and walked out of the vegetarian's paradise. Their walk back through the valley was a peaceful one. Along the way, Breech looked at his watch and noticed something funny.

"Hey, Dunaway!" interrupting Anuk and Dunaway's conversation, "What does your watch say?"

"It says," rolling up his protective sleeve, "I've got twenty after two."

"According to our watches, we've only been in the garden for forty-five minutes."

"That's impossible, mate. We've been here for at least five hours."

~ XVII ~

The three stopped walking as Anuk started laughing silently, but not silently enough. The two stunned scientists looked at their friend questionably before asking, "Anuk, what's so funny? You knew this was gonna happen, didn't you?"

"Yeah, mate, what gives?"

"Time exists differently in the garden."

"Differently? You said that once before. What's different about it there?"

"There are no words for it, except different. The effects will not last long."

"Effects, mate?"

"Time, energy and motion, Professor..Physics 101." Anuk smiled really big and started walking the path back to the winding ridge out, leaving his two new friends staring at each other with baffled looks on their faces. As the three moved through the forest, Breech asked Anuk if the time structures would last long.

"About two days."

"Two days?!"

"Yes. The effect will subside slowly."

"Dunaway," Breech started in a professorial tone, "Do you think a magnetic field in this area caused our watches to malfunction? That could be a cause for the giant fruits."

"Don't forget radiation, mate."

"Oh God, not that."

"We'll know more day after tomorrow when we get back to our lab site."

Anuk laughed lightly.

"Now what, Anuk?"

"You will see."

Moving toward the valley ridge, they noticed the path was a little clearer than they remembered coming through the first time. When they reached the canyon wall, they noticed the path ridge leading out was also clearer.

"Holy, Mary! Look at the ridge steps, Breech." Breech, trailing in the rear now, stepped into view.

~ XVIII ~

"Holy Mary's right my friend. It looks as if fifty people cleared the way out."

"No magnetic field or radiation could've done this, mate."

"No, definitely not." Anuk chuckled lightly again.

"Now Anuk, you're not gonna tell me you were expecting this to happen, too."

"You will see many strange things for a short time."

"Yea, like what, mate?"

"Look at your watch." Both scientists checked their timepieces and found out they had reached the ridge two hours sooner than it took the first time.

"Good heavens!" Dunaway exclaimed.

"Unless my watch is slow, we're two hours ahead of schedule." Anuk smiled as he started up the makeshift stairs out of paradise valley. On the way up the steep, winding ridge, Professor Dunaway noticed something odd about his pack.

"Hey, Breech," who was now trailing second, "Is your gear getting lighter, or am I having a stroke here?"

"Yeah." He said looking over his right shoulder, "Come to think of it, it is. We can check everything when we get to more stable ground."

"Sounds good to me."

They reached the top one at a time. Then the three men stared silently over the enormous valley for several minutes.

"Well mates, she's a beautiful site." Dunaway's voice cut the silence like a well-sharpened knife. They knew it had to end.

"We've got cargo to check and a bit of a walkabout ahead of us," he continued.

"Next full moon," Professor Breech quietly commented, "next full moon."

Coming out of the canyon should have been exhausting, but it wasn't. All three men should have been sweating profusely, but they weren't. It was as if they just strolled out to the end of the driveway to get the morning paper.

"Mr. Dunaway, Anuk was right about one thing."

~ XIX ~

"An' what's that Mr. Breech?"

"This trip is definitely different. This rucksack of mine feels like it weighs about five or six pounds. But I know I've got a good sixty pounds of supplies inside."

"Well, we'll know if they've turned to air shortly, mate," Dunaway commented as they made their way around the wooded ridge. When they reached level ground, all their supplies were grounded. They started opening their packs and pulling out cargo to find that nothing had changed. The banana still weighed 2 pounds and the grapes were still fresh and heavy as well.

Then Professor Breech noticed something. He picked up a bag with several large size fruits together and it was light as a feather.

"Heavens!"

"What's wrong, mate?"

"Feel this," as he passed the bag to his partner.

"It feels almost empty."

"See what I mean. Take something out and see what happens." He reached in and pulled out the cantaloupe, almost bowling ball size, and it was heavy. The rest of the bag of fruit got a little heavier.

"I don't know what to think of it," replied Breech. "It's as if . . the more . . fruit you put together . . the lighter they get."

"Breech, that contradicts every law of physics I've ever studied."

"I know my friend. But you're seeing this with your own eyes."

"Unbelievable, I see it mate, but I still don't believe it."

"Yeah. We've got some work to do when we get back to the lab."

"You can say that again. Let's get packed back up." They looked over at Anuk as he was smiling brighter than usual.

Breech stared at Dunaway and said, "You know, he's enjoying this."

"Yeah mate," he answered, grinning. "I can see that."

After a couple minutes of repacking, they were once again on their way. They trekked on until they reached another point of reference.

"Look mate! There's the twin tree again."

~ XX ~

"That's impossible," Breech stated as he looked at his watch. "Hey, Dunaway."

"Don't tell me Professor. We're ahead of schedule again."

"By almost three hours."

"Bloody hell," he replied, examining his watch and then looking up at the afternoon sun, "What's going on around here?"

"Well," Breech started, "let's keep moving. We're getting close to our first camp site, aren't we Anuk?"

"We are closer than you think. We can set up camp a little further up," Anuk smiled widely.

"Yeah," Breech said, looking him in the eye, "you're having toooo much fun with this." Both men smiled as they joined Professor Dunaway at the base of the hill where the beautiful twin tree stood.

"Isn't she stunning?" Dunaway commented.

"Yes, very much so. Are you going to get some samples?"

"Not this trip, mate. I think we've got our hands full already."

"Well, it's your call, partner."

"We could finish our tests on what we've got first, then she'll become our next project."

A short time later, they reached their original campsite. And, after grounding their gear, the scientific minds started smoking. "I can't for the life of me figure out why we're making twice the time getting back. There's no scientific reason for it. The Native Americans taught me as a child that the earth has many energy centers. These vortexes can sometimes play tricks on time and space. Some people have claimed to have seen past battles at these energy sites. But . . . this time barrier has gone on for more than a few moments. What do you think, Dunaway?"

"Well mate, the Aboriginals back home say that time only exists for those who wear watches."

"And what do they say about the sun that keeps the same time?"

"Follow the universe Professor Breech, just, follow the universe. After all, there's not a bloody thing we can do about it. And besides, who's going to know about this but us?"

~ XXI ~

"So what you're saying my outback friend, is 'Don't worry,
be happy.' huh"
"Now you got it, mate." The two visitors of the rain forest
prepared camp while Anuk hit the local stream for their evening
meal. The scientists refused to eat any of their newly stocked
supplies until they had done a few tests in their lab. They were
both a little worried that there might be some radiation in the
food. After all, it's not often that one sees bananas as long as a
human arm. With the sun fading over the warm jungle hills, the
scientists whistled while they worked.
"You know mate, we'd better get that fire started soon.
You know it doesn't take Anuk long to catch dinner."
"That's the truth. I'll bet it wouldn't take him long to win a bass
fishing contest back in the States." Both men chuckled while
they gathered wood. The day ended with three full bellies and a
cozy evening fire.
    The next morning began with coffee and leftover catfish.
"What time you got, mate?" Dunaway questioned with a smile.
Breech, on instinct, glanced at his watch, and then looked back at
his partner.
"We're not going through this again, are we?"
Dunaway and Anuk laughed aloud.
"Now you're both having fun at this." Breech said waving his
finger at both of them.
    It only took a few minutes to gather up and start back
toward the village. After an hour into their journey, they could
see the large hill that rose skyward next to their destination. Soon
after, their home was in sight. The closer they got, the more they
could hear the children laughing and the voices of the tribe.
Walking into the village, they noticed some sort of ceremony
being prepared. The children did not run out to greet the three
travelers as they usually did. In fact, only the elders and Ranu
came close enough to greet them.
"Anuk, what's going on? What are they doing? They've gotten
the night fire started early." Breech wondered as the elders were
walking toward them carrying three wreaths of small flowers.

~ XXII ~

"It is a cleansing ceremony."

"For us, mate? Why?"

"A person that returns from the badgood place has to be cleansed." Anuk respectfully bowed his head for the elder to place the wreath around his neck. Not wanting to offend their new friends' tradition, both scientists bowed their heads as well. The elders said a few words and then went back to tending their fire.

"Anuk," Breech whispered, "how long do we have to keep these things on?"

Anuk smiled. "Until the ceremony is over."

"And how long will that take?"

"About 1 hour."

"An hour?!" Both Westerners gasped. "We better put our things away. Oh, by the way Professor, it took us a little over a day to get back, when it took almost two and a half days to get there. What does your scientific mind have to say about that?"

Stowing his gear away carefully in the lab, Dunaway turned to Breech and began singing: *"♪Here's a little song I wrote, you might want to sing it note for note♪...?"* At this point, Breech joined in. *"♪Don't worry . . . be happy, don't worry be happy now . . . Ooooh ♫...?"*

Some of the villagers started laughing and pointing.

Anuk came over and told the team that it was time to begin. "We can unpack the rest later. We'll still have plenty of light."

"Let's get this over with," Breech replied heartily. A short discussion with the elders after the ceremony led the two to believe that the fruits themselves were harmless. It seems that most of the elders, spread throughout the forest, have eaten the fruit at one time or another. It was the secluded 'blue pear tree' that caused restlessness in the minds and hearts of the people here. Many campfire nights, the villagers had overheard the elders talking about the mysterious garden. There were more questions than answers, again.

With the help of Western science, just maybe some of those answers would come to light. Having several hours of daylight le the two scientists walked over to their jungle lab to begin their tests. The first test they did was to check for radiation in the various fruits. The tests came back negative. In fact, they have never seen more nutrient-rich plant life.

"I don't believe this!" Breech commented. "There are more vitamins and minerals than a dozen of their kind back in the States."

"Yeah, mate. A body could stay healthy forever eating this stuff."

"Where's the small bag the pears were in?"

"Right there by the monkey," he answered, pointing toward the lab entrance. Breech walked over to their furry mascot to pick up the bag.

"Holy cow! This bag's heavy."

Dunaway looked in his direction. "It's just fruit, mate."

Breech opened the bag and encountered the surprise of his life.

"Dunaway, look!" He pulled out one of the fresh pears to find that it was not so fresh.

"Bloody hell!"

"They're hard as rocks, petrified even. Anuk! Come quickly!"

Anuk ran to the lab to check out the commotion.

"Look at this!" Breech showed him the fruit, the petrified fruit.

Anuk smiled. "Yes, badgood."

"Is this the mystery the elders spoke of?"

"Yes. Many questions, no answers."

"Anuk, this can't happen. Fruit just doesn't turn into stone in a twenty four hour period. We can't even do the right tests on these."

"We're not set up to do any geological studies, mate."

Anuk continued to smile, as usual. "Later you will see."

"See what?" Michael Dunaway was very intrigued.

"It will live again."

~ XXIV ~

"You mean to tell us that this will be fruit again?" Professor Breech was on the edge of his seat holding up a stone pear.

"It can't turn back into fruit once it's been petrified."

Anuk looked him in the eye and said, "It cannot turn into stone in twenty four hours either . . . no?"

"He's gotcha there, Breech." Laughter echoed throughout the camp as one scientist laughed at the other.

"Well, when? When will it turn to fruit again?"

"No one knows. An hour? A day?"

"We'll just have to wait and see then, won't we?" Breech turned to Dunaway and let out a sigh.

He smiled back at his partner, saying, "You know, we may have found the discovery of the century here. It may even be the fountain of youth."

"What? How can that be?"

"First these bloody things were plump, juicy pears, blue mind you, but pears just the same. Now, these things look older than dirt. They're petrified. Think about it. We just have to figure out how and why it changes so quickly."

"I'm not fully convinced yet that they will change. I mean, these things could probably only survive and keep fresh while on the tree. It's certainly gone through a drastic change once, but I can't see how it's gonna change back to the way it was. That's impossible."

"We can wait to cut one open when they do change. Or, we can use a chisel to get inside."

    The day was ending as John discussed the impossibilities of what they had discovered with the elders. Then, right around fireside time, Dunaway yelled, "Breech, come here!"

Like a cat, Professor Breech bolted toward the lab. "It didn't!"

"Bloody hell, it did!"

Breathing heavily, Breech reached into his pocket and pulled out his knife.

"What are you gonna do?"

~ XXV ~

"I'm gonna cut a slice off so we can examine it before it changes again."

"Be careful with the pit. I wanna try and plant it."

"You'd better be careful yourself. I don't trust this thing . . . at all."

After cutting a piece off, they noticed that it had the same texture and moisture as other pears they were accustomed to handling. The only odd thing they could physically see, aside from its changing properties, was its shiny, blue skin and rather large size. It was slightly bigger than pears found in American or Australian markets. Breech cut off a smaller piece and walked over to the table next to the microscope. He reached in a semi-sterile cloth pocket and pulled out a surgical knife. He then sliced off a very thin layer, placed it on a slide and put the remaining piece on the table to his right. He began to examine the specimen under different magnifications while his partner carefully removed the pit. The house monkey, nicknamed Airam, was perched over Professor Breech watching all the excitement. He also saw that remainder of fruit lying on the table. As Dunaway carved the fruit to extract the seed, he asked how the light analysis was going.

"You know Breech, this thing might not even gro. . . The monkey!" Breech looked to his left at Dunaway, who was pointing to his right. "The monkey got the fruit!" he yelled, scrambling to his feet. Breech glanced immediately at the table to find the piece of fruit gone. Looking up in the rafters, they saw their mascot examining his 5-finger discount. The fruit thief finished it off as the two watched in awe.

"What do we do now, mate?"

"Wait 'til he turns into stone, I guess."

"I'm usually the comedian here."

"Well," Breech said, scratching his head, "I guess we'll have to keep him under observation while we do our tests. I don't know what else to do. I'm at a loss."

~ XXVI ~

"Well mate, it's a new one on me . . . a stoned monkey."

The evening continued with numerous tests done on both the soil and the strange fruit. Anuk was also curious to see what would happen to the monkey as the three kept an eye open for anything strange.

As the evening campfire lit up the village, the elders questioned the three explorers about their findings. Since most of the natives were fearful of the garden, no one would go near the lab since they returned. Tests showed that all the fruit was edible. Of course, the three sojourners had to eat it in front of everyone to prove it. Several questions were still unanswered. What about the blue pears? Why do they turn to stone? Are they dangerous?
Also, what will become of the monkey? The scientists assured the elders that they would have more answers by the next sunset. They also told them of the great nutrients that the fruits and vegetables contained. The elders agreed that having good food to eat for their people was deserving of celebration. Exchange of good friendship and cozy talk went on while Breech excused himself to check the lab. A moment or two went by before he was heard. "Dunaway, come quickly!"
The professor bolted toward the lab with Anuk closer than his shadow.
"What is it?"
Villagers started talking as the elders stood and watched in silence.
"Your seed! Look!"
"Bloody hell!" The three stood over the seed that Professor Dunaway had planted in his homemade potting soil. Only it was no longer a seed. It was a two-inch tall plant with a stalk almost as hard as tree bark. Anuk called over to the elders to let them know what had happened. They smiled back, waved, sat down, and resumed talking.
"They don't look too impressed." Dunaway declared.
Looking back down at the plant, they scooped it up and put it on the table.

~ XXVII ~

"Anuk, has anyone been in the lab?" Breech asked.

"No, no one has come near since we returned."

"Can't say I blame 'em, mate. I mean, look at this. This has to be the strangest living thing on earth. I just planted this thing less than 4 hours ago . . ."

"Yes, I know. It's growing at a rate of a half inch per hour. Where's the monkey?"

"He is up there." Anuk gestured to the bamboo rafter.

"Little guy hasn't moved since he ate that piece of fruit. He just watches everyone as if he's tryin' to figure us out. Blimy, I hope he's gonna be alright." Dunaway worried.

Anuk pointed to the table. "Look there."

"Dunaway, can you believe it? The pear has petrified again!"

"Look at that." He picked up the remains of the pear they had cut open for testing and it was still fresh.

"What's going on here? None of this makes any ..." A small ding cut his sentence short. The lab's small, battery operated toxicology machine had finished the test before their fireside gathering began.

"Now," Breech started, "now we'll see what's in this odd fruit."

"What is it?" asked Dunaway. "If it's poison, the monkey would have shown some symptoms by now."

"Most assuredly, let me see," Breech said quietly, reading.

"Oh my God."

"What, mate?"

Looking back up at Airam on the rafter, Breech said, "Maybe he is trying to figure us out."

Anuk and Dunaway looked up at the monkey, who was staring down at them, when Dunaway asked, "What did you find?"

"Do you know what peyote is?"

"Yeah, some aboriginal medicine men use a similar plant in ceremonies. It shuts down the conscience mind and allows a person to see through their unconscious, like dreaming while wide awake."

~ XXVIII ~

"Yes. The Native American medicine men use it for ceremonies too. Well, this has the same exact chemical composition of the 'hallucinogens' in peyote . . . only three times more potent. This stuff will allow a person to see into the unconscious mind."
"The little guy must be going out of his then."
"Or maybe he has gotten smarter. This day has been too much for me. I'm hittin' the hammock." Breech walked over to his swinging bed, reading the rest of the test results.
"Well, it has been a long one for me too."
Anuk smiled, said goodnight in his native tongue, and walked back toward the fire.

The two awoke the next morning to the laughter of children.
"What in the blue blazes is so funny?" Sitting up, Breech saw the monkey holding a glass vial and putting it in the proper container. The monkey caught the doctor of science watching him and quickly climbed back up onto the rafter.
"What were you doing?" He said, rubbing his eyes. "Don't get into our things, you little . . ."
"What are you babbling about, mate?" Dunaway said as he was stirring. "What's so funny? Why are the children laughing?"
"Professor, you better have a look-see."
Breech was fully awake now.
"Look-see what?" Rolling over and sitting up, he noticed that the lab was clean, not spotless, but a lot cleaner than the exhausted scientists had left it the night before.
"Who the . . . Anuk! The two checked to see if anything was broken or missing.
Anuk stepped into the lab. "Did you need something?"
"Who cleaned the lab?" Dunaway asked, pulling on his shirt.
With the children laughing and pointing in the background, he explained that he had just returned from a morning 'glory walk' to find things to teach to the older children.
"I have not been here." Then, turning to the children standing on a very large log, he asked in his native tongue who was in the lab. The children laughed and pointed at the monkey.

~ XXIX ~

Anuk grinned halfheartedly at the doctors then looked back at the children who were still giggling.

"No, not in the lab. Who cleaned the lab?" He repeated in his native tongue.

A few of the children laughed while all of them pointed at the monkey and said, "Watchusa," the monkey.

The three adults looked at each other for a moment and then slowly turned their eyes to the little furry guy sitting on the rafter. They stared at him and he stared back. Breech slowly waved at him. He quickly waved back.

"I saw him put a glass test tube in the metal rack when I was waking up." Anuk left the two wondering so he could continue to talk to the children, who were still watching.

"No bloody way! You are not gonna tell me that that little monkey cleaned up the entire lab. Mind you, it's not very big, and we left a little mess last night. But wild monkeys do not clean up after humans!"

"Ha ha ha!"

"What's so funny, mate?" Dunaway asked in a fury of disbelief.

"I'm usually the one upset. ♪*Here's a little song I wrote...*" Breech began singing.

"Oh, knock it off." Dunaway smirked. Anuk walked back in.

"The children say that after I left this morning, before sunrise, the monkey started cleaning, first himself, and then the lab."

"Makes no bloody sense."

"Why doesn't it?" asked Breech.

"What? Are you mad?"

"No, listen to me," Breech grabbed Dunaway by his shoulders and smiled while talking. "Don't you get it? The fruit . . the monkey ate the fruit. He didn't go out of his mind. He got smarter. He's found new brain cells to use."

"I dunno. If he's smarter, how come he doesn't try to communicate with us?"

"I believe he is . . . in his own way."

~ XXX ~

"This stuff won't kill 'im, will it? I mean, you did say that it's three times more powerful than peyote.""This level shouldn't be harmful. The tox test I did showed it pure and clean of any deadly chemicals."

"He looks happy," Anuk interjected, smiling.

The monkey smiled back at the three men staring up at him. All three smiled back as Dunaway held his arms up to him.

The furry, lab mascot hesitated, scratched his chest with his left hand, then climbed down into the professor's arms.

"I guess the little guy was scared we'd get on to him for touching our lab equipment."

"Well, we did get on his case quite a few times before."

"What do we do now, mate?"

"Let's find out what he can do." Looking around the lab, Breech noticed something. "Dunaway, look at your plant."

"The bloody thing has grown half a foot!"

Sure enough, more leaves and branches had grown at an incredible rate.

"Dunaway, ol' chap, it looks like you've got a Jack-and-the-beanstalk situation on your hands."

"Yea, no kiddin'." With his small tape measure in his hand, Dr. Dunaway proceeded measuring the height, width, and number of new branches. "This thing is growing over three quarters of an inch an hour now. We'll have a full-grown tree in ten days. Wow."

"Wow? Is that a scientific term, my aged, outback professor?"

"Hey, I'm not that much older than you. Besides, in a month's time we'll have a tree older than the both of us."

Making full use of their time, they worked with the monkey as much as they could. They were not quite sure when the effects of the exotic fruit would wear off. They had one experiment using a deck of playing cards that fascinated them. They could give him a card and he would put it on a pile of the same suit.

He put hearts on hearts, and clubs on clubs, without missing a lick.

"Breech, you've found yourself a new spades partner."

~ XXXI ~

"Yeah, maybe we can get him ready for Vegas."

Hours went by. The plant continued its rapid growth and the monkey games were astounding. He could draw simple shapes, recognize letters and numbers, and even follow commands they taught him.

"This lil' bloke is smarter than any chimp I've ever heard of."

"I'll say, if he could only talk. I wish I knew what was going through his mind right now."

"He's probably thinking, 'Hmm, humans really are strange creatures.'" Both men chuckled.

"No doubt. If we could teach him some sign language, we could probably understand him better. But I don't know any si..."

"I know some, mate."

"Really?"

"They actually taught this in school growing up in Australia. I liked it so much that I took a course later on in college.

"You've never said anything to me about signing."

"Guess it never came up. He's very smart right now. He should pick up on simple things like 'man' and 'monkey' but might have trouble signing letters."

Later that evening, just before the campfire was lit, the monkey was in the lab signing something to Breech.

"What is it, boy? Hey Dunaway! What's this furry genius signing?"

"Oh! It's time to eat. He's hungry. Maybe you ought to get him to teach you sign language, Breech." Dunaway poked.

"Very funny. Come here, boy. Uncle John will get 'cha a bite to eat."

Right after the campfire, the two scientists returned to the lab to find a pile of long small vines in the center of the floor.

"Jesus! I thought it was a snake coiled on the floor." Breech jumped with surprise as he was the first to step into the lab.

"What is it, mate?" Dunaway peeped around his partner's shoulder. "Well, who do you suppose did this?"

~ XXXII ~

The monkey was chattering up above them and hitting his wrists together.

"There's your answer."

"Is that communication, or is he trying to hurt himself?"

"He's signing 'work', but I don't know what he means."

Dunaway signed back, 'What work? What do you want?'

The monkey climbed down from his rafter, walked over to Breech's hammock and started shaking it.

"No bloody way," Dunaway replied faintly.

"What is it? What does he want?"

"He wants us to make him a hammock too."

"You've gotta be kiddin'."

"Look at him. He even brought the correct sized vines to do it with. I told ya he was smart."

The little guy then walked over to the pile of vines, picked one up, and hit one wrist on top of the other.

"Well Professor Dunaway, it looks like we're in the hammock-making business."

A short time later, Anuk walked in on the two scientists sitting on the floor making something while the primate watched curiously

"What are you making?"

The two scientists looked at each other and just laughed.

"A very small hammock mate," Dunaway replied looking over his right shoulder.

"For who? The monkey?"

"Yes," Breech answered, looking at him with an odd smile. Anuk started laughing out loud.

"What's so funny mate?"

"First monkey worked for you, now you work for monkey...very funny."

"What would really be funny would be if he could actually make this thing himself," Breech grinned.

"Yea, the bloke just likes watching us do it."

The three men stared at him as he smiled very big, as if understanding every word they said.

~ XXXIII ~

The two men chuckled as they continued their job. After almost an hour, the hammock was finished and hanging from the bamboo rafters. The little Capuchin monkey climbed up into the hammock on his belly,looked down at the two, and grinned from ear to ear.

"I guess that means he likes it."

"Well mate, I like mine, too. After a brief cleaning up of my own, I'm gonna introduce myself to it. I'm startin' to feel a little drained."

"I know what 'cha mean. I've had enough excitement for one day. You go ahead and clean yourself up, and I'll take care of our mess here."

"Thanks mate, I won't be a minute."

Professor Dunaway was the first to wake to the jungle birds' morning songs. "Hey, Breech?"

"What?"

"Wake up."

"I'm awake Aussie."

"No, you're not. You only call me that when you're bloody tired. Wake up."

"Why?"

"You didn't clean up the lab last night, did you?"

"No. Why?"

"Neither did the monkey,"

"What?"

"I believe the effects of the fruit are wearing off."

"What do you mean?"

Dunaway started walking around the lab, looking. Glancing up at the monkey on his hammock, he noticed something.

"You see, look at the little guy."

"He looks normal to me."

"Look at the way he keeps eye contact now. It doesn't last as long." Dunaway replied as he stretched his arms up to him. He climbed down into his open arms and wrapped his furry arms around his neck. "The little guy hasn't lost his affection."

The two men talked, and then started tests to find out how much knowledge he had retained. To their surprise, he remembered quite a few sign gestures, eat especially.

"Well mate, it looks as if the effects on him lasted just a little over twenty-six hours, depending on when it wore off last night."

"It's kinda strange, don't 'cha think?"

"What's that mate?"

Looking up at the little hammock and pointing, Breech began, "He still enjoys his hammock."

"What's strange about that?"

"Well . . . he enjoys his, just as much as we do ours, but he didn't know how to get one. How much other stuff do we do that he doesn't know how to ask to do himself?"

"Huh? Say that one more time in English mate."

"Okay, look. When we were lying in our hammocks, he wanted one to lie in, too. So, how much other stuff do we do that he would like to enjoy, but he doesn't know how to ask?"

"So, you're saying we should teach him to do experiments?"

"No, no. Not experiments really, just planting seeds and mixing soil."

"We could keep an eye on the little booger to find out what keeps his interests."

"Agreed. He may know more now than we expect."

"By the way Breech, why did you name him Airam?"

He grinned very big before he spoke. "I have a wonderful ex-girlfriend named Maria."

"Maria?"

"Airam backwards"

"Ooooh … OK. Do they look alike?"

Breech's big smile returned.

"Naw, the monkey's a lil' taller."

The scientists shared one of many smiles together as they started the day with a new student in hand. Approximately two hours later Breech yelled, "Dunaway! The pear has changed back!" He rushed over to the lab with Anuk close behind.

~ XXXV ~

"Well, what do we do with it now? How many times is this thing gonna change?"

"Mate, we're no closer to solving this mystery than we were when we found it."

"You can say that again. What if we were to prick the skin of the fruit to see if that will stop it from changing? The other one didn't change when we cut a piece out of it. Maybe this 'un won't either."

"The only thing that will bloody prove is the fact that we would know how to stop the metabolic change that it keeps going through."

"But we will know then why it stops changing. Either that, or wait for it to turn back into a rock."

"Or maybe, one of us should try it mate"

"You mean eat it, like Airam?"

"Why not? There are only so many tests we can run on the blamed thing. Other than watch the tree grow at a fantastic rate, what can we do?"

"We don't know the full effects of what might happen."

"We've already tested it on our lab animal, so to speak. He's doing fine. Look at him. Except for the few things he can do now, he's back to normal."

"You're half crazy, you know that?"

"It'll be like going through an Aboriginal ceremony."

"Let me make an antidote just in case. It won't stop the induced coma, but it will bring down the effects some."

"It won't be that bad, mate. You'll see."

"You really are an adventurer, aren't you?"

"Hey, no guts, no glory."

"Agreed, but I will keep full surveillance on you. In the one book, I'll record everything, including your own emotions and thought patterns. Got it? And, in the other book, we'll record nothing at all."

"Sounds like a plan. When do ya wanna start?"

~ XXXVI ~

"We could start first thing in the morning, at sunrise. That way we can crash out early tonight for a fresh start tomorrow."

The two scientists kept only one journal between them about the secret garden and its contents. Since the place was sacred to the people here, no one in the world would ever read about this part of their South American journey. Their personal journals were for anyone in research science to read. These people were both kind and nurturing to others and nature. The scientists were going to do everything possible to keep unwanted attention out.

The anticipation of their next experiment was greater than going to the forbidden ground. They prepared everything for the next day just as evening fire was being lit. They told the elders of the next morning's plan and that they would have Anuk give them hourly reports. All the elders began talking at once, to each other. The two scientists looked at each other strangely. Did they say something to offend them? Breech looked at Anuk.

"Anuk, I don't understand what they're saying. They're talking too fast."

"They are talking . . ." The elders stopped speaking. Then the eldest spoke up, slowly. "He says there needs to be a purification ceremony."

"For who mate?"

"You, mostly."

"Ah, because of the fruit." Michael nodded in agreement. "Yea, well, let's get on with it."

Twenty to thirty minutes later the two were on their way back to the lab. Airam was glad to see them. As soon as they stepped in, he climbed down out of his hammock and into Breech's arms.

"Hey, you miss us? He certainly has become affectionate since his little adventure, hasn't he?"

"Definitely, I think it was in him all along. It was like you said, mate. He just didn't know how to communicate with us."

"We've got a long day ahead of us tomorrow. I'm going to bed. Go over to Uncle Michael, he'll put you to bed."

"Come here Airam." After a few minutes of quality time, Professor Dunaway retired as well.

The two faded off to sleep with the jungle sounds and people talking and laughing around the campfire.

Michael Dunaway awoke with his chest feeling a few pounds heavier.

"What the . . Oh, good morning Airam. Did you sleep well?" He signed as he talked. The monkey signed back, 'sleep no.'

"You no sleep?" Airam pulled the sheet off his chest.

"Oh, me no sleep." He laughed aloud.

"What's so funny?"

"The monkey says it's time to get up."

"Oh, great. Now he's talking."

"Only with his hands, mate."

"How does he know we wanted to get up early?" Breech replied in a half-sleepy voice.

"Maybe he wants some of that bright, shiny pear fruit."

"Well, when he asks for it by name, then I'll give it to him, and not by signing." Professor Breech talked, yawned, and stretched all at the same time.

"Let's get a bite to eat before we send you into la-la land."

"Ha! You're really dreading this, aren't you?"

"I still think you're nuts for doing it."

"Well, I haven't done it yet."

"You mean you're having second thoughts?"

"No way mate. One fact the Aboriginals taught me; Fear cannot hurt you. It's only a feeling. You feel hot, you feel cold, you feel fear."

"Yeah, let's see if that logic works later." They looked at each other and smiled as they put their blankets away.

About that time, Anuk walked in.

"The elders wanted to know when you were going to begin."

~ XXXVIII ~

"Tell 'em right after we've had something to eat. Professor Dunaway needs to put something on his stomach first."

"Are you nervous?" Anuk asked.

"More anxious than anything," Dunaway smiled back.

After the natives started using the spices that the professors had made with the jungle herbs, roots and flowers, their morning meal of fish had become more enjoyable.

After breakfast, the elders, scientists, Anuk, his trainee, and the tribe alpha female, Asil, got together for a short 10-minute ceremony. It was kind of like a spirit booster, like going to church one night in the middle of a busy workweek. The eldest took a stick from the morning cooking fire and blew the loose ambers and ash off.

Dunaway kneeled in front of him as if being knighted by a king. The elder then, while talking, encircled his head and shoulders with the smoldering stick. Then, Asil handed the elder a small wreath of small white and yellow flowers she had made the night before. He placed it around Michael Dunaway's neck. He stood up, a few words were said, and the ceremony was over.

Anuk walked back to the lab with the two men. Breech went over next to the main table, opened a cloth sack that had the remains of the pear, took it out and gave his partner a piece.

"Down the hatch mates," Dunaway said, smiling while chewing.

"What's it taste like?"

The professor twitched his eyebrows up and down. "It's like a pear, only much sweeter . . . like honey-dew mel . . ." A serious look came over his entire face as he slowly chewed.

"What is it Michael?" Breech asked with a concerned tone.

"It's . . . it's like nothing really matters." he said slowly chewing in a quiet voice.

"What do you mean nothing matters? Everything matters."

Looking directly into his partner's eyes, he reponded,

"No, you don't understand. Life is balanced to take care of itself."

"Yes, that's true, but what about the fruit? How do you feel?"

"I don't know . . . how to feel. It's as if my feelings are strong, but aren't very important, the way I'm dressed, the way I look, the temperature . . . doesn't really matter."

"Dunaway, you're starting to babble. What about your thought patterns? What are you thinking?" Breech was starting to get frustrated.

"We have time," Michael stated. "My thoughts . . .
aren't really mine."

"What do you mean?"

He turned his head and smiled at his partner as if he didn't have a care in the world.

"John, it's like there are a billion thoughts out there and we only choose the ones we want to dwell on." Anuk stood in silence as he listened to the two men.

"There's knowledge everywhere!" Dunaway laughed aloud.
"I feel like a 200lb weight of worry has been lifted from my shoulders."

"I'll bet you do. I'm gonna let you stew a while so I can write a few things down. Just relax and get yourself together. We'll talk shortly."

"No worries mate." He replied grinning from ear to ear.

"For you maybe." Turning around, they faced their silent partner.
"It's okay Anuk, you can talk to him. I was right. He's only half crazy."

"Anuk ol' fella, how are you, my friend?" He laughed aloud.
"I am not as happy as you." He replied grinning.

An hour later Anuk and Dunaway were slowly walking around the campsite area.

"Don't go far," Breech said loudly, "I want to keep an eye on you."

Dunaway smiled back without saying a word. In fact, as time went on, he wasn't saying much at all. He was telling Anuk that his English words were not what he was trying to express.

"Too many words, adjectives ... get 'n the way. They just don't work." The professor barely got the words across.

~ XL ~

"Why?" Anuk asked.

"The words are lazy and vulgar."

Anuk spoke a few words in his native tongue. To both men's surprise, Dunaway was answering and understanding. It was slow at first, then got a little easier for him.

Fifteen minutes later, Breech heard a laughing commotion coming from the camp area. He looked over and saw Anuk and Dunaway talking to the elders. He went over to see what was going on.

Walking up, he heard his Australian friend talking, not in English, but in excellent native tongue.

"Dunaway, that sounds brilliant. I don't remember that much from my lessons." He turned and looked at Breech, then spoke. "Speak no English."

"What do you mean, speak no English?"

He started speaking native tongue again.

"I don't understand but a few words. Tell me in English."

Dunaway stopped for a moment. He was moving his lips but nothing came out. He turned to Anuk and spoke, and then Anuk spoke to Breech.

"He says his mind is on a different level. Speaking English makes him dumb."

"Dumb? Why?" Breech questioned.

Dunaway spoke again. Anuk translated, "He says it is easier to understand, but hard to speak."

"Why is it so hard to speak your own native tongue?"

"It...is..dirty." Dunaway uttered.

"I'll admit that our language has many glitches in it, but that's no reason not to speak it." Breech smiled in confusion.

Dunaway spoke in native tongue and smiled.

"Anuk, what did he just say?"

"He asked, 'Would you drink dirty water or beer?' "

"Ah, it's a deep mental choice. But, I still don't understand why your language is easier for him to speak."

"It is not easier. Do you not understand?"

"No, not really."

~ XLI ~

"English is a clear clumsy path through the jungle, with many obstacles."

"So you're telling me that he is challenging his mind, making it work harder, on purpose."

"Yes, to him English is like an old toy a child does not want to play with anymore. Philosophy 101." Anuk smiled.

"Anuk, you're a man among men. You could've been a doctor."

The small group of men sat down around the campfire pit and talked. The two scientists learned more about these peaceful people today than they had all the other days combined. They learned of their flight from the valley garden. They also heard the horrific story of thousands of villagers dying by the clumsy hands of American scientists and Christian missionaries with common colds. The elders split the tribe up into seven different groups and spread them throughout the jungle to prevent the annihilation of their culture. This happened twenty to thirty years before Anuk was born, so he only knows of the smallness of his people now.

The elders seemed to be a lot more open with one of the scientists speaking their language now. The conversations went on until it was time to light the nightly fire.

Most of the tribal fears faded with meeting and talking to Professor Dunaway after he had eaten the mysterious fruit. It would seem to most that science had defeated superstition. However, to these people, it was just a part of life's lessons.

After returning to the lab, Dunaway found it a little easier to speak English. "John?"

"Welcome back." Breech chuckled.

A blank look of expression crossed Dunaway's entire face as he slowly sat down. Tears filled his eyes.

"What is it? Are you sick?"

Shaking his head no, he turned his pale blank face toward his friend. "It . . just hit me."

"What hit you? What's wrong?"

"The fruit . . . the garden ..." as if to force the words out.

Breech spoke, "What's wrong with the fruit?"

~ XLII ~

"Don't you get it?" He asked.

"Get what? You made more sense to me speaking their language."

As if tears were going to flow, he replied, "I ate the fruit. We went to the garden."

"Yes, now you're making some sense."

"And at the entrance of the garden, God placed two angels."

"That sounds like the book of Genesis for crying out loud."

"Yes, it does."

A ghost-like expression came over Breech's face as he slowly sat down whispering. "Holy God, we found it, didn't we?" Dunaway looked into his eyes and slowly nodded in agreement. "We found the Garden of Eden, and we can't tell a single bloody soul." Dunaway's voice faded as the two men sat in silence, a silence that lasted almost an hour.

"What are we gonna do?" Breech asked.

"No one can read our journal. Every scientific and religious nut case in the world would show up here. No mate, no one can ever know about this."

"I agree. Everything here would be destroyed. Should we burn the one journal?"

"I think we should keep it to ourselves. We might need it someday."

"Oh no." Breech's eyes lit open. He turned his head and pointed. "What about our new fruit tree?"

"You're right. It's about two feet tall now. We'll have to make a trip back to the garden and replant it."

"We'll have to do it soon, or we'll need an ax to cut it down first. I just can't believe it. We found the Garden of All. My Sunday school teacher would flip." Breech laughed aloud. Just then, two strangers walked into the camp area. They had been sent to deliver a package to the science team. Inside were a few supplies and a picture of the flowering plant they had originally come here to find. Dunaway began chuckling.

"What's so funny now?"

~ XLIII ~

"The lab obviously thinks this," holding up a picture, "would be a great, rare find. We have the discovery of the world with that garden and they want us to look for this."

"Remember, they don't know about this."

"I know mate. I'm just joking."

Anuk walked up as the two were rummaging thru their care package. "Mailman come?"

"Yes," Breech answered. "And we have a few things to show you. First, this."

"Ooh, toilet paper."

"And finally, this," showing Anuk the picture. He recognized it immediately. "This is what we came here to find."

"Yes, it grows high on the hillsides."

"Mate, you're telling us you've seen this?"

"Yes, it is on the mountainside, on the way to the garden."

Both scientists laughed.

"Anuk, we need to find this plant. And, depending on how Professor Dunaway here feels tomorrow, we need to make another journey back to the garden. Our new tree is gonna have to be replanted there."

"Yes, I understand. I will tell the elders."

"What do you think about us burying our journal there where no one can find it?"

"Sounds good to me. You could bury it next to the badgood tree."

"Yeah mate, we obviously can't carry it back to the States with us."

"Then, tomorrow we get this tree back, bury the journal, and get what we came here for. The next day we'll go find your Australian plant, as soon as the elders give the okay that is."

"I think they will approve." Anuk smiled at his two new friends. "This has been a fruitful journey, huh, mate?"

"More than the world will never know, my friend . . . more than anyone will never know."

~ XLIV ~

Needless to say, the West Virginia lab was enthusiastic about the results of the science team's expedition. The two men were awarded bonuses for their efforts. The Australian government was also very appreciative of the men's discovery. Moreover, Dunaway, well, let's just say he now finds it easier to study and speak different languages.

Until next time . . . The End

-Healer-

The morning started out for little Billy, like so many others, with his mom getting him up and ready for his farm chores. The family had a small fifteen acre spread in the rolling hills of Kentucky. At twelve years of age, farm chores, or any chore for that matter, seemed to get in the way of fishing, playing in the hay loft, or spending time with his best friend King, the family dog. Wherever Billy went, the Great Pyrenees was always by his side.

"Son, hurry up. Breakfast is ready." His mother, Joyce has been his alarm clock all his life. Though she is a petite woman, that has never hindered her from taking on the large tasks expected of a farm wife and mother. His father, Bill Sr., is old school to the bone. 'If it don't work, use a bigger hammer.' Both parents are in their mid forties and have been married for a little over fifteen years. During their marriage, they had talked about having children for quite a long time but were unable to do so. When Joyce finally did get pregnant, it became the greatest blessing they could ever hope for. They wanted their future child, or children, to grow up in an atmosphere that would teach them things about life that no school education ever could. So they moved out of the suburbs of town life into the country.

The smell of bacon and eggs filled the modest two-bedroom country cottage as Billy walked into the kitchen. "When you get through eatin'," his dad started, "you need to hurry up and feed and water the animals and don't take all day about it. We've gotta fix the corner fence in the hayfield. I wanna turn the cows loose in there after the second cut." It was normal for a farmer to open the hayfield for grazing, to rotate the cows for easier feeding in late fall.

"Bill, is he gonna have time this afternoon to help me pick the sticks up out of the yard so I can . . ."

"Nooo. We've gotta get the fence fixed then check the rest of the line"

"Okay, okay. I just wanted to get the yard mowed before it gets dark."

"That yard can wait. We've gotta get this haven't found that missing cow."

"Which one's missing, Dad?"

"That little girt you raised. She's been gone since yesterday morning sometime."

"Bessie's gone?"

Mom started setting the table just as the biscuits were finished cooking. The blessing was said. Breakfast was eaten, and the day was on.

With the temperature and humidity both in the mid seventies, the day's chores were a little easier to deal with.

That evening after supper, Billy wanted to go fishing in the back pond. He and King walked around the barn lifting up boards and rocks trying to find enough worms to fill his old coffee can.

"Here's a jackpot, boy." He told his 120 pound best friend.

"We've got enough now. Let's grab our pole and catch some fish."

Petting King, he stood up and walked to the garage to get his tackle and light. A short five minute walk to the back field was well lit by a full moon and a clear starry sky.

"It feels like a good fishing night, huh boy." He sat down on the pond bank. The reflection of the moon off the water's surface was almost blinding. Billy baited his hook in anticipation.

"You think we'll catch Ol' One Eye tonight, buddy?" King laid beside him, looking up every once in a while in acknowledgment.

"That big ol' catfish is going home with us tonight. Look how big that shootin' star is. It must be our lucky night."

Young Billy was excited as he made his first cast into the pond while staring at the night sky.

"You know boy, that's the largest shooting star I've ever seen. It even looks like it's getting bigger. King!"

Boooom! A short time later the excited young man was running toward the house. A worried mother and father were outside trying to figure out where the noise came from.

"Mom! Dad! Did you see that?" He asked as he was climbing over the gate into the yard.

"Son, are you okay?" His father asked.

"Yes sir. Did y'all see that?"

"What was it?" His mother asked as her worry subsided.

"A shooting star landed close to the pond. It scared me and King to death."

"Let's go take a look." His father said boldly.

The family grabbed up a couple of lights, loaded them in the pick-up truck and headed toward the back field. Reaching the impact site, they found a crater over 200 feet long and three feet deep. From the truck's headlights they could see a twenty foot wide hole in the fence that had been ripped and burned away.

"Mercy, Bill." Mother softly said.

"It's a sight ain't it?" He replied.

They all got out to inspect the damage.

"Good Lord, look at the size of this hole!" Father exclaimed. They could hear sirens in the far distance.

"Wait'll the newspaper gets a look at this."

"Why Dad?"

"Son, not too many meteors actually make it to earth. Most burn out when coming into our atmosphere. Most do, but this 'un didn't. Where were you when it hit?"

"I was over there," pointing toward the opposite side of the small pond. "See? My pole's still in the water."

With small ambers of fire and smoke still rising from the crash site, the family walked around and examined the damage. The sirens got even closer.

"I don't see any fragments left from it." Bill stated.

"Should there be any left?"

"Yeah Hun there should be something. The ground is warm everywhere. Son, what did you...Son? Both parents looked around, not noticing that he had walked back over to his fishing spot.

"Son, what are you doing?"

"Fishing, Dad."

"Don't you want to see this?"

"Why? It's just a hole in the ground."

Bill looked at Mother as she smiled and repeated, "It's just a hole in the ground."

They shared a laugh just as sirens and flashing lights appeared in the family's driveway. A cluster of automobiles, including county police, and the Milton fire and rescue turned off their sirens as they drove into the cow pasture lighting up everything with red and blue flashing lights.

"Get away from there!" The deputy yelled getting out of his unit.

Bill and Joyce got in the truck and backed away from the site. They parked beside the deputy and got out.

"Why?" Bill asked.

"This site could be radioactive," the paramedic stated.

"Oh, Billy!" Mother gasped. Husband and wife ran toward the pond.

"Wait!" The deputy yelled chasing after them.

From where everyone was parked, little Billy could not be seen behind the high pond bank. Though he was over 400 feet away from the impact site, parental fear saw no distance.

"Billy," his father was the first to reach him, "Leave your fishing gear. Let's go."

"Why, Dad?"

"The crash site may be contaminated."

"Dad, there's no harm there now."

"Why, Son?"

"It's clean." Billy calmly stated.

Mother reached them with the deputy close behind.

"Folks, this is a pretty safe distance, but nonetheless, let's just get to the vehicles."

"I agree," the father said.

Grabbing the lantern, bait bucket and tackle box, the three adults waited for the youngster to reel in his line. Suddenly, the pole bent straight over.

"I've got something!" Billy yelled.

"Reel him in easy," the father said.

"Boy, that's a whopper," claimed the deputy.

"I'll bet it's Ol' One Eye," the boy said excitedly.

"Take your time," lessoned his father.

This tug-of-war between country boy and fish went on for almost five minutes. Pulling it within inches of shore, his father stepped to the water's edge and helped his son pull it out. It was him. This catfish was approximately three feet long. It was almost solid black with a very large head, a prize catch for anyone who likesd to fish.

"Where's your scales Son?"

"In my tackle box, Dad."

"The guys at the station won't believe this."

"You finally caught him." Mom smiled as she ran her fingers through her son's hair.

"Aww Mom, not in front of the guys." Lil' Billy was slightly embarrassed as a few of the men chuckled.

"Ah, here it is."

"Bill, I've gotta camera in my glove box." The deputy trotted toward the flashing lights. More sirens started sounding in the distance. He was returning to the pond as the catch of the day was being weighed. He could hear laughter and cheering.

"How much?" The deputy asked as he worked on catching his breath.

"Eleven and a half pounds," the father exclaimed.

"Wow! That's a monster. Let's get a few pictures. I'll give these to Mavis at the drug store tomorrow morning. She'll get 'em developed and back to me by lunch time.

This might even make the paper! We've been here long enough.
We should probably move over to the vehicles."
More sirens could be heard in the distance.

"More people are coming?" Joyce asked.

"Yes." The paramedic replied.

By now, ten people were standing next to the pond watching the
youngster's prize catch getting taken off the hand-held scales.

"What're ya gonna do now?" The father asked his son.

"Let 'im go," he replied.

"What?" his mother started. "After all this time, you're
gonna let him go?"

"Well," he said, "we've got pictures and witnesses. Why
keep him?"

"That's an adult decision." His father smiled.

"One more picture with the whole crew?" The deputy
asked. "Witnesses and all should do."

Everyone got together and smiled for the camera. He then
released the catch of a lifetime.

"I hate to bust up a good time folks, but we need to head
toward the emergency vehicles."

With Ol' One Eye free and back in the pond, everyone walked
slowly back to the bright flashing lights in the field. Sirens still
made themselves known from afar.

"Who else is showing up here?" Joyce asked.

"That's probably Kentucky emergency. They'll tell us if
the site is contaminated or not."

"Why would it be contaminated?" Joyce inquired once again.
The sirens died out as they too entered the Roach family farm.

"The state people will be able to tell you more than I can."
Three more vehicles pulled into the field. The deputy went to greet
them. Two men got out of a large white van, talked to the deputy
for a few seconds, then climbed into the back. Minutes later they
came a few seconds, then climbed into the back. Minutes later
they came out wearing silver colored suits with hoods.
One held a machine of some type that looked almost like a
miniature metal detector. The deputy walked back to the family
and medical personnel to tell them what was happening.

"What are they doing?" Joyce asked as she held her son.

"They're checking for possible radioactive contaminates."

"Oh mercy." She worried.

"It's gonna be alright ma'am," the deputy assured. "This is just a precautionary measure. They said that sometimes there's a low radiation level when meteors make contact with our planet." Bill put his arm around his nervous wife.

"Are we gonna be okay?" She asked.

Billy looked up at his parents and said with a smile,

"It's gonna be alright. You'll see."

His mother patted his smiling face, and said,

"I'm sure it will, sweetie."

After about a very long five minute sweep by the silver-suited men, one took off his hood and seemed to smile with relief. He turned to the small waiting crowd of people, nodded and grinned. The other man took off his hood, kneeled down, and took some soil sampleThe man with the detector walked over to the now relieved crowd. "Well, folks, I guess you can tell everything is alright, but I still need to check you individually." He took a hand-held device clipped to his suit and waved it over everyone. "Was there anyone else around the site?" He asked while clearing the last person. "Not when we got here," the medic claimed. Father said, "My son was here when it hit."

"King was with me," Billy exclaimed.

"Yeah, where is King?" Dad asked.

"He high-tailed it toward the barn when it hit the ground."

"We need to check him just the same."

"Let's head toward the house. My son'll call him out to you." At the barn next to the house, Billy went into the hay room and turned on the light.

"I knew you'd be here." King was curled up like a puppy on the thick hay floor. His dark brown eyes veered toward Billy. He growled a low tone, showing his teeth.

"Hey boy," Billy said gently. "It's still me, buddy."
He extended his hand to the now quiet, gentle giant. King sniffed him, slowly wagged his tail, and then went in close for a Billy-hug.

"You see, boy. I'm still me." Wagging his tail frantically, he licked Billy on the side of his face.

"That's my boy. There's a man out there that needs to look at ya for a minute. Come on, boy."
The two friends trotted out of the barn to the waiting crowd. A minute later, one of the men reassured the crowd, "Well, it looks like everything's okay. You folks are gonna be just fine."

"See boy," Billy said, bending over to hug his hairy best friend, "I told ya everything's fine."
The good-nights were said, and everyone except the Roach family prepared to leave.

"We do want to take a better look in the daylight tomorrow."

"Come back anytime," Bill said.

"Y'all be careful." Joyce waved as she went arm in arm with her son into the house.

The next morning began a little earlier than usual thanks to the town newspaper and a city news crew. By lunch time, it seemed like half the town's population came out to see the meteor crater. The family dealt with the attention, and soon one by one everyone went back to their places in life.

Two weeks later, the family got their lives back. Bill walked into the house to fix himself a sandwich for lunch.

"That new calf ain't gonna make it."

"Oh, poor thing," mother replied.

"Once they go down, they don't get back up. I was gonna give that pretty thang to the 4-H kids at school to raise."

"Are you sure you can't save him?"

"It's a she, and I've done everything I know how to do. She won't make it through the night."

"Does Billy know?"

"Yeah. He's out there with 'er now."

"I'll call 'im for lunch."

Sticking her head out the door she yelled, "Billy!"

"I'm in the barn!"

"Come and get a bite to eat!"

"Okay! I'll be there in a minute!" Five minutes later he walked in the back door a little exhausted.

"Wash ya hands and . . . oo, you look tired."

"I feel tired, a little. Dad, I think that calf is gonna be alright."

"I wouldn't get my hopes up, Son. We'll see at feeding time this afternoon." Bill gave his wife a silent 'no' headshake as Billy was walking out of the kitchen toward the bathroom.

At feeding time, just before dark, Bill walked into the barn to drag the dead calf out and was amazed to see her on her feet, and hungry. He stood there speechless.

"That's impossible," he said to himself. The calf was as perky as a pup.

"Yeah! You're gonna be alright." The father was smiling and shaking his head left and right when he walked out of the barn.

"What's wrong, dear?" Joyce asked him as she was bringing out the trash.

"That calf I thought was gonna die . . . is still alive."

"I believe our son said it would be okay, didn't he? She smiled mischievously.

"Just like our meteor crash, he said everything would be okay." The smile faded from Joyce's face. At that instant, they looked around for their son.

"Billy?" Mom called.

"I'm over here." He rounded the chicken pen with King. The four came together in front of the barn.

"Son," Dad started, "What happened to the calf?"

"I don't know. I sat with 'er for a little while talkin' to her. She just stood up." He shrugged his shoulders slightly and spoke with understanding eyes, "She was happy after the talking to."

"The Lord works in mysterious ways," Mom smiled.

"Yeah," Father said, "but this is beyond what we're used to."

"Don't question miracles," She added.

"I know, I know," he slowly nodded.

"Supper's almost ready. I'm just waiting for the biscuits to get done."

"We'll be in in a minute. Son, finish feedin' the chickens and check their water. I'll bottle feed the calf."

"Okay, Dad."

The next morning, Billy was up and out doing chores before his mom and dad awoke. Dad was drinking his morning coffee when Mom went to wake him.

"Billy, Son . . ." She stepped into his room. "Son, it's time to . . ." She walked back toward the kitchen. "Bill, he's not in his room.

"I know," he said quietly holding his coffee while gazing out the kitchen window.

"How did you know?"

He turned to his wife and put his index finger to his lips.

"Shhh."

"What is it?" She asked.

"Look." He whispered pointing to something outside. Their son was sitting in the yard rubbing King's belly. Butterflies and sparrows covered him and the ground around him.

"Oh, Lord," his mother whispered. "I'm speechless."

"Wait and see," he replied.

A few seconds later the boy turned his head and stared at the kitchen window as if he knew he was being watched. Instantly, the insects and birds scattered as if a cat was about to pounce on them. The parents' and son's eyes met as though a benevolent energy had come between them. He smiled at his parents as they stared at him in bewilderment.

King sat up and looked around as if a wolf had entered his domain. He growled and barked twice.

"What do we do?" questioned the father.

"Smile back," she replied. Billy could see their lips moving, and their questionable smiles. He smiled back and petted his best friend without missing a beat.

About a week and a half later, on a Saturday morning, excitement hit the Roach farm. The farmer next door, Tom Ellis, came barreling up the gravel drive in his pick-up. Billy and his father ran to meet him.

"Bill, I need your help. I've got a yearling heifer stuck in the pond."

"Billy, go inside and get the horse blankets."

"Yes sir."

"Tom, help me get a few things."

A few minutes passed and the three were on their way. Pulling up to the barn, Tom got out and climbed on his tractor. Father and son drove to the back pond to find a 300 pound Black Angus calf stuck up to its belly in clay mud.

"Grab all the straps out of the back." Bill instructed boldly as the noise of the tractor approached. Tom drove his John Deere to the edge of the pond while Bill strapped the calf's harness on. The spring-fed pond was cold and mud-cloudy from the bovine's struggling. His toes went almost numb in seconds.

"Lower your bucket!" He yelled over the diesel engine. "Son, hand me the end of that strap!" After another couple of minutes the young calf was pulled from the cold, clay-muddy water.

"Let's put 'er in the back of your truck!" Bill hollered. Tom nodded yes and moved the big green Deere backwards slowly while the calf kicked furiously. Mud and pond water were slung all over Billy and his father. He turned the tractor off so he could hear his neighbors' voices.

"Stay back, Son, don't let 'er kick ya. Let 'er settle down a bit, Tom. She's hoppin' mad right now." She stood to her feet after a few tries. She was freezing from the frigid waters.

"Have you got an open stall we could . . . Billy, stay back." Bill caught his son reaching out to pet the mentally unstable animal.

"It's okay, girl." Billy rubbed a circle or two on her forehead. The calf stopped struggling and gave a healthy "Mooooo."

"I'll be . . . would you look at that?" Tom was dumbfounded. Billy was hugging the cow's neck and brushing cold mud off. Billy started taking off the straps.

"Dad, can we have a blanket?"

"Sure, Son."

He reached in the back of the truck and grabbed the horse blankets. He brought them within three feet and the heifer started walking sideways and mooing.

"Okay, okay," Bill backed off.

"Better let me do it Dad."

"Well, that's gratitude for ya. Who do you think was in that cold water with you?" Bill started smiling and looked at Tom who was still on the tractor and shaking his head in disbelief.

"I'll explain later." Bill told him. "Tom, did you say you had a stall open?"

"Yeah, last one on the left when you go in. Lights are on already."

"Good. Billy, Son, lead her toward the barn."

"Are you sure that's safe, Bill?" He watches his son lead her past the truck, and then looks back at Tom.

"Yeah, Tom, I think it'll be alright." He smiled as he turned toward the pick-up.

Back at the barn, Bill and Tom started running some extension cords to hook up a couple of heat lamps, while Billy got the poor, cold calf settled in.

"I sure hope this thing lives." Tom told Bill as they were running the cords.

"I was surprised she was able to walk. And darned if I can figure out how your son was able to calm 'er down like he did." Bill stopped walking. After a couple of steps, Tom stopped and turned to face Bill, who now had a very serious smile on his face.

"What is it?" Tom questioned.

"That's not all, Tom."

"What's not all?"

"...At our house too."

"What?"

"Billy's been healing and settling down animals all over our place."

"What do you mean?" He took a slow step toward Bill.

"Joyce and I thought it all started with that meteor that hit our place a short time back."

"Yeah. Everyone remembers that. That space rock put our sleepy lil' town on the map. Sorry, go ahead. What were you sayin'?"

"We were all tested by those state people and the medical personnel. They ran several tests and found nothing wrong with any of us. Animals that were supposed to have died, lived. Tom, I had a calf in the last stage. It started with her gettin' the squirts, to not eating, to lying down struggling to breathe.

Billy was in the barn with her for about a half hour. A few hours later I went in to drag her dead body out, and she was up eating grain."

"Are you sure she wasn't just . . ."

"Tom, I know it sounds weird. Joyce and I dismissed it once or twice, but, well, you saw it with your own eyes."

"What are y'all gonna do?"

"What can we do?" Bill finished unrolling his cord while the conversation faded. When the two men reached the barn stall, they were only a little surprised when they saw the calf up on her feet feeling perky.

"Well, I'll be . . ." Tom muttered.

Bill turned to him and grinned. "I told ya."

"You . . could call the news?"

"Oh please, people still come by to take pictures of that blamed hole in the ground, a 203 foot long hole in the ground." Tom laughed out loud as Bill's voice diminished.

"Do you really want all those news crews back here?" They smiled at each other.

"No, I guess not." Tom agreed.

"Son, you 'bout ready to go?"

"I need just a few more minutes with 'er, Dad."

"Alright. Holler at me when you're ready."

"Okay. That's a good girl." Billy dried her off and petted her till it was time to leave.

Four years have passed. Only a dozen people or so, outside of the family know about Billy's special gift, a gift that has gotten stronger. He only spent about ten to fifteen minutes with a sick calf before it started showing improvement. He had all the animals timed. A sick chicken took three to five minutes to heal, a dog five to ten, male goats fifteen to twenty, female ten to twelve. For years, he has been keeping records on all the animals he helped. He wrote down whose farm, the sex of the animal, what type of animal, how long the process took and their progress.

He'd planned on being a veterinarian, and he had more going for him than just a good bedside manner. He was making straight A's at school. At almost seventeen, he was the top varsity baseball player, not to mention they were headed for state play-offs. Their biggest rival, the Couchville Dawgs, were to be played twice by the end of the season. The first of the two games would be played this Saturday, at home, in Oakland Park. The coaches drilled and grilled their teams all week. Billy's school only went a half day Friday to assist the ball team with practice. The coach wanted to work on plays and go over a few things without anything strenuous. Their team was tied for first with Couchville. Though both teams could lose this Saturday's game and it wouldn't really hurt them, as long as they didn't go on a losing streak. All the other AA teams had three or more losses each.

Saturday morning: It was chores, then breakfast. There was no such thing as a vacation if you lived on a farm. Every morning and evening animals have to be fed. The game was at two, but the team meeting was at one. That left plenty of time to do what was needed to be done around the homestead. Billy found that thirty minutes of fishing around the pond before a game helped to relax him and keep the stomach butterflies at bay. King, naturally, joined him.

Three and a half hours later, the whole family was on their way to the 'Duttenmater Game', so nicknamed by the players because it 'doesn't matter' if either team lost; it wouldn't do any damage. This was nothing but a way to size each other up for the play-offs.

There were about sixty people in the bleachers when the home team took the field. They worked the ball around a short time while the coaches got acquainted. The umpire stepped behind the plate.

"Cougars, you ready?" He looked at home team.

"Dawgs. You ready?" He looked at the visitor's side.

"Let's, play ball!" The crowd cheered as the first player stepped up to bat.

Both teams played like it was a championship game. At the bottom of the second inning it was tied three to three and the Dawgs were at bat. So far it had been a real cat and dog fight. The coach's son was on deck as their power hitter was up to bat. With two men on, he stepped up to the plate. The first pitch was low and away for the Dawg batter. The second was a little outside the box, but he took it. Driven fowl toward his visitor's side in a blur, the coach's son didn't see it in time. The ball hit him just below the temple under the rim of his helmet.
He fell as if there were no life left in him.

"Will!" The visiting coach yelled.

"Time!" The ump shouted, throwing his hands and arms up in the air.

The crowd gasped as both coaches ran to check on him. His
teammates started gathering around the unconscious player.
One of the town's doctors, whose grandson was playing, came
out of the stands to assist.

"Don't gather around. Let some air in."
He got down on one knee to check his eyes.

"Call an ambulance, now!" The doc yelled.
He was checking his pulse when Billy started walking in from
center-field. As he stood to the side of the crowd, he dropped
his glove and slowly lifted his hands and stared at his palms.
He then looked up into the bleachers where everyone was on
their feet. Joyce had one hand over her mouth and was holding
her husband's arm with the other. Billy and his father's eyes
locked as Bill nodded yes, slowly. Billy, stared back at his
hands, smiled a little, then turned and walked through the crowd
to the injured player. He knelt beside him as his father
approached from behind through the same hole.

"Step back Billy," the doctor stated.

"Doc," Bill started, "give him a minute, would ya?" Billy
put one hand on the injured player's chest and one on his forehead.

"What're you doin'?" The concerned father asked.

"I'm not real sure. This works on animals at home."

"What works?" The doctor asked.
Billy fell silent as the ambulance wailed into the parking lot.

"His pulse is getting stronger," the doctor claimed.
One minute later, Billy lifted his hands.

"I need some cold water.
The injured player opened his eyes.

"You shouldn't give him water just yet," Doc stated.

"It's not for him, it's for me. Feel my hands." The doc
put his hands on Billy's palms then quickly pulled them back.

"Wow. They're hot. Why?"

"The negative energy is gone from him now."
Billy half-smiled.

"Dad?" The injured player, Will, started speaking.

"You should take it slow, son. I'm Doc Weathers, one of the town's physicians."

"What happened, Doc?"

"You got hit by a foul ball. How do you feel?"

"A little woozy, but no headache." He groggled.
The medical personnel walked onto the field.

"Let's get you to the hospital for an X-ray." The doctor motioned for the paramedics. "This young man needs a cranial cat scan for a possible concussion."

"You got it, Doc."

They slowly walked him to the medical unit. Most eyes turned toward Billy, who was rubbing his hands together under a water spigot. The team coach for the Dawgs was the first to approach him.

"I don't know what you did, but I want you to know, I'm very grateful. I'm Coach John Lampley. That was my son Will that you just helped." Billy turned off the water and wiped his hands on his uniform. They shook hands.

"I'm Billy Roach. That's my father Bill over there, coming this way. Mom's . . in the crowd somewhere up there." The doctor and umpire walked up on the two talking.

"Billy, what happened? What did you do?"

"I'm not real sure, Doc." He answered with a puzzled look on his face still trying to dry his hands.

"He's been able to heal animals on the farm for quite some time." Bill toned from the small crowd.

"I felt his pulse get stronger." The doctor opened his hands while talking. "The medics will see that he's gonna be alright."
The Dawgs coach joined in, "Thanks to you, young man." He put his right hand on Billy's left shoulder.

"It was nothin', Coach. I really wasn't sure if it would work on people. I guess I never considered it an option."

"Billy, if I can ever do anything for you, let me know."

"Well, Coach, you could start by finishing the game."

"I'm game. Coach, how 'bout you?" The visiting coach asked the other.

"I'm ready! Ump?"

"Let's play ball!"

The home team was tied at the top of the fourth with bases loaded. Billy, who had the highest batting average in the league, hit a grand slam. The coach's son, Will, had showed back up at the bottom of the eighth. His mom picked him up at the emergency room after a few head shots by means of X-ray, cat-scan, etc. He showed up in the stands with his team jersey draped across his shoulders. He gave his coach and team two thumbs up. The final score was Milton Cougars eleven, Couchville Dawgs seven.

Billy and Will met after the game and exchanged numbers.

"Your dad a pretty good coach?"

"Yeah," he said looking back over his left shoulder,

"Dad's an alright coach."

"He seems alright to me. I like 'im."

"Billy?" Coach Lampley questioned as he joined the two players' conversation.

"Are you gonna be ready to do some fishing tomorrow?"

"Well, I'm supposed to help my father do some fencing."

"I talked it over with him, and if you and Will help get it done early enough, you'll be able to toss some lines in."

"I'm gonna help?" Will asked.

"Yeah, Son. Your mom said the doctors told her you had no restrictions. I hear Billy here likes to fish as much as you do."

"That sounds cool." Will said smiling.

"Well?" The coach looked at Billy.

"Sounds just fine to me." He seconded the motion with a smile.

"Alright, it's settled, tomorrow it is. I'll drive Will over around seven so you two can get an early start."

"Yes sir," Billy smiled.

The three were walking away from each other when Will
stopped and turned around.

"Hey, Billy!"

"Yeah?"

"Good game!" He smiled to almost a laugh.

"Thanks, you too!"

The Roach family was returning home when Bill asked,

"Where do we go for a victory dinner? Mother?"

"Don't ask me, I was in the cheering section." They both
stared at their smiling son.

"I would like a Shoney's hot fudge cake."

"Shoney's it is." Dad chuckled.

The next morning was met with some anticipation; a new
farm hand for a day, not to mention a new fishing buddy. It
should be a different Saturday nonetheless. Will and his father
pulled in the drive at twenty till seven. The Roach men were
busy doing a few small chores before breakfast. Joyce came out
to yell for her two favorite men to come eat.

"Oh, good morning Coach, good morning, Will."

"Morning. Please, call me John."

"Alright, John. You two wanna biscuit? Breakfast
is ready."

"No thanks," he responded. "We've eaten already."

"How 'bout some coffee, then? You and Bill can talk."

"Coffee sounds great."

After breakfast, over coffee, the conversation was sure to
come up.

"So Bill, Joyce. . . I remember you saying that Billy has a
gift he uses to help animals?"

They looked at each other and smiled.

"He has a gift with animals. He can sense them as much
as they can sense us." Joyce commented.

Bill spoke up smiling with, "He can spend some time with
an animal that is dying and . . . well, we haven't had one animal
in over 5 years on this farm to die of an illness."

The coach looked at Billy and questioned,

"How do you do this?"

"I don't really know. It felt a lot different with Will than it ever did with the animals."

"Why? What was different?"

"With Will, it felt like my hands were transferring a tingling energy, and at the same time they were taking a negative energy out of him. It was like I was balancing his soul." The room got quiet for a moment.

"You've got a miraculous gift. If our dog gets sick, I'll bring 'im to ya." Everyone laughed.

"I'll let you folks get to your farm work. I'll pick Will up around dark."

"Sounds good," Bill claimed.

"Work him hard, he needs it."

"Aw, Dad!"

"We'll be sure he earns his lunch." Bill assured him.

"Now your dad's on me."

"It's an older generation thing." Billy countered.

"I'll older generation you in a minute. Will, while you're here, make yourself at home. Billy can show you around before we get started."

"Thank you, Mr. Roach, I'll do my best."

"Sure you will. Billy, when you're through showin' Will the ropes, so to speak, load up the fencing supplies on the trailer and hook it up to the red tractor."

"Yes sir, come on Will. Lemme show ya the barn."

"Make sure the tractor has fuel and oil, too."

"Will do."

As the two athletes walked toward the barn, Will's curiosity turned into words.

"So let me ask you something. How many animals have you helped with your gift?"

"I don't really know. I have a journal with everything written down. Maybe thirty animals on this particular farm."

"Wait a minute. You've helped other people's animals, too?"

"Sure, I helped Widow Lackey across the road, Mr. Ellis next door, and ... well several other people in this area here that have needed me."

"How come everyone doesn't know?"

"The only thing I can figure is, there are two possible reasons; one is that people aren't really sure that anything even happened, and two, that too much publicity would wreak havoc on a small town community." He ended with a slight snicker.

"So how many people have you helped?"

"Every time I help their animal, I help them."

"That's not what I mean and you know it. How many people have you healed?"
Billy held up one finger.

"You're the only one."

"Does that make me a guinea pig?" The two laughed as the barn doors swung open.

By 3:30, both major fields were finished. Perfect weather and all the homemade lemonade you could drink ended the day.

"Let's get back to the house and do chores, and back the wagon into the barn. You two should have plenty of fishing time after that," Bill said.

"Oh, yeah!" They agreed loudly.

The day was done, now time for fun. Billy showed Will his favorite worm hole. Out behind the barn under the old black tarp was a catfish's paradise.

"I've got several good places for bait, but this is my favorite." Billy pulled back some barn boards and black tarp covered with cedar shavings.

"Wow!"

"I told ya. Jackpot!"

"We've got enough here to fish for a couple of days!" Will said grinning.

"We don't do much around here on Sundays except for the usual feedings. Why don't we see if you could spend the night?"

"Yeah! We could fish into the night."

"Woooe, slow down. We need to get the adults to go along. . ."

"Billy! Will!"

"Yeah Mom!"

"Where you at?!"

"We're behind the barn!"

"Do you want Will to stay the night?!" She could hear them laughing. "Now I wonder what was funny about that."

"Well?!"

"Yeah, we're gonna fish tonight. Did you call his dad?!"

"Yes, I just got off the phone with him!"

"Thank you, Mootheer!"

"You're welcome, Soo-oon!"

"How about that for timing?" They laughed.

"She must've been talking to my dad when we came up with the idea. What a coincidence!"

"Aw, Will," he started as he was pulling the black tarp and board back over its spot, "There's no such thing as coincidence."

"What do ya mean?"

"I mean there's no such thing as coincidences or accidents. Everything that happens is supposed to whether we like the results or not."

"What about me getting clocked by that ball yesterday?"

"You got a fishing buddy out of it didn't cha'?"

"Yeah, I guess I did." He smiled.

Under a full moon, the two boys fished until late in the night. They were sitting beside each other when Billy broke the silence between them.

"It was a night a lot like this when that meteor crashed into that fence row over there. Man, that was a crazy night. I was about 12 years old at the time."

"Wow! I remember that. Your farm was on the news. I didn't know it was you. You guys had news crews all the way from Nashville up here."

"We didn't, that meteor did. It's my turn to ask you something, Will."

"What?"

"So what did it feel like yesterday? I mean, from the time you were hit until you woke up. What do you remember?"

"Nobody's really asked me that. All anybody asked me was how do you feel and is anything blurry. When I got hit, I felt pain, pressure, and darkness. When I woke up, it felt like the first breath of air I ever took. All fear left me, like . . . a shadow running from sunlight." He turned and faced his new friend with a serious look. "What did you do to me?"
Billy shrugged his shoulders.

"It's like I took the negative energy out of you. To me, it felt like heat was moving with a tingling sensation in my hands and wrists . . . guinea pig."

"Ho! Very funny."
They laughed aloud as Billy continued.

"It felt different with you than it did with any of the animals. Even though I was removing the energy from you, it's like it wasn't even me that was doing it. I was just there being used."

"Used? You mean like God?"

"No. Nothing is forced, it...just happens naturally."

"What? I don't understand. What do you mean, naturally?"

"You can't ring a bell. You can hit it, but the bell rings on its own."

"Yeah, but you made it ring."

"One merely hits it. How long it rings is up to the bell."

"Like an echo?"

"Yeah, exactly."

"I kinda understand." Will said, still a little puzzled.

"Logic and common sense won't work. It's beyond all that." Billy smiled.

"That's too deep for me."

"Me too, really. I try to feel and not think. It's a lot easier." Billy chuckled. "I'm just glad I met ya. No one likes to fish as much as I do. You can come here anytime."

"Thanks, I probably will."

As time went on, the two became the best of friends. However, when it came to baseball, they were on opposing teams, and they knew it.

And, a short time later they proved it. Just as most people expected, the AA state game was between Couchville and Milton. Both teams had incredible records, including players and coaches. Another cat-and-dog face-off was expected. The Couchville ball players knew that Billy had an almost perfect batting record. They also knew he was the miracle player that helped the coach's son. Since he and Will had been hanging out together, they also knew of his unique ability, or what they believed to be true. His batting ability was the only thing to fear from him.

Since the two schools were only about twenty-five miles apart, the park in Couchville was packed. Billy and Will got to talk a minute or two before things got started.

"Hey Will. Your park here looks great. You ready to play?"

"Ready as I'll ever be. How's your batting average?"

"Over 400 so far. No strikeouts this year."

"Wow!"

"Remember to feel, not think." Billy encouraged his new friend.

"I'll try."

"Good luck, and watch your coconut."

"Count on it. "

"Coach is ready. Talk to ya after the game."

"See ya, good luck Billy"

The game went back and forth. Very few errors were committed by either team. They all played like professionals making million dollar contracts.

In the end, only one team could be the winner.

Final score: Couchville Dawgs 13, Milton Cougars 11.

Even Billy's perfect batting game wasn't enough.

During the after-game presentation, the Couchville team was having a huddle without their coach. Will, the team captain, asked them, "Are you sure you guys wanna do this?"

"We're a team, aren't we?" The pitcher commented. Coach Lampley walked up to the team huddle.

"Are you guys ready to thank the other team?" Everyone quietly turned and looked at their coach.

"What's the matter?" He asked.

"Dad, Coach, you know we wanted this trophy more than anything."

"What's wrong?"

The first baseman spoke up. "Coach, you got us here. You should choose where the trophy goes. We're a team. We've won the championship and no one can take that from us."

"What are you guys trying to say?"

"What we're trying to say, Coach, is, well, Will wouldn't be here with us now if it hadn't been for Billy. We know that." The coach's eyes watered with tears.

"I understand." He choked the words out.

"Like we said, Coach, it's up to you."

"Thank you, boys. You've shown more heart here today than all the players combined that have ever played this sport. I'm very proud of you, all of you." As a tear rolls from his left eye, the coach said, "Let's do this." He turned and walked to the opposing dugout where family and friends were gathering. The team walked quietly behind him.

"Coach Babcock."

"Yeah, Coach Lampley."

Picking up the 1st Place Trophy, he spoke.

"I . . . scratch that, we, would like to present your school and team with this first place trophy." The entire crowd, team, officials and umps became deathly quiet.

"I don't understand."

"We believe this player right here," placing his hand on Billy's shoulder, "is responsible for saving my son's life. This is just our way, in good sportsmanship, of saying thank you."

"Well, I'll be. I don't know what to say." The coach was almost speechless.

Billy's mother, along with others, came to tears.

"Can they do this, ump?" Coach Babcock asked.

"It's a first for me," he commented, "but I'm just the umpire. You'll have to ask the officials here."

"It's gotta be a first in American history. No winning team has ever given away their trophy to the other team. But, it doesn't change the championship, just the location of the trophy, Do what'cha want." The official stated.

"It's your's now."

"We will proudly display this in our trophy case with your school emblem on it."

Everyone in both cheering sections, both teams and even some officials cheered aloud.

"Then it's settled." Coach Lampley declared.

"Thank you, Coach. I think we've just found ourselves a sister city."

Bill, who was standing close by, said "Hey coaches, why don't you bring both teams out to our house for a weenie roast next Saturday night?"

"Coach Lampley, what do ya think?"

"Sounds great to me."

"Next Saturday it is." Coach Babcock agreed.

The weeks rolled by until one day the Roach family got an unexpected visit. Two cars came up the driveway, one of which they recognized. It was Will and his mom and dad. The other car had two fairly young adults in the front and a child in the back wearing a ball cap. Billy and his father came out of the barn to see who was there.

"Hey, Will!"

"Hey Billy! How y'all doin'?"

"We're just tryin' to work on the barn gates."

"Hi Bill."

"Hey John, how are you?"

"Fair to partly-cloudy, I guess."

"What brings y'all out?"

"Bill, I'm sorry to come out unannounced."

"Ah, don't worry 'bout that. You guys are always welcome."

"Well, thank you. Bill, Billy, this is Terri and Taylor McCanless. And this little lady is their daughter, Laura." She looked to be about nine years old, a little thin and weak, and the ball cap covered a completely bald head.

"We're here . . ."

"I know why you're here," Billy interrupted. He got on one knee to see eye to eye with the frail child.

"Hello, Laura. My name's Billy. How are you?"

"My tummy hurts."

"I'm sorry, sweetie." He smiled at her.

"Can you help our daughter, please?" Terri, spoke almost in tears.

"I don't know, ma'am, but I'm willing to try."

"We've tried everything," the father stated. "The chemo doesn't seem to help much."

Billy stood up.

"Lemme wash my hands right quick, and we'll see what we can do."

As he walked to the barn washroom, the visitors explained their situation.

"For the past year and a half after we found out Laura had cancer, we've been just about everywhere and seen every specialist. Everyone wants to help, but it's a constant uphill battle. She'll go into remission for a few weeks, and then it'll start all over again. John here was telling us how Billy helped Will."

"Taylor, right?" Bill questioned.

"Yes."

"Taylor, he's been able to help animals. But, Will here was, well, I don't want you to get your hopes up."

"Like we said," he looked at his wife's worried face, "we're just trying everything we can no matter how farfetched it may seem to people. We're very desperate."

"My son'll help if he can."

Billy walked back to the group as the conversation ended.

"We're not expecting positive results. We've been dealing with this long enough to know not to do that."

"Hi, sweetie. Where's the problem at?" Billy questioned.

"Just under her stomach in the upper colon," the mother stated. Billy was on his knees when he took off her hat.

"Would you hold this, please?"

He handed it to her father.

"This won't hurt at all."

"What are you going to do?"

"I'm gonna use my hands to feel your tummy, okay?"

"Alright." little Laura whimpered.

Everyone got quiet. The mother, teary eyed, folded her hands together under her chin and leaned into her husband's arms.

"That tickles."

"What does, sweetie?" Billy wondered.

"My tummy feels like bugs."

"Like bugs?" He asked.

"Yes, they're walking on the inside of my tummy." After about 3 minutes Billy removed his hands off her stomach and lower back. "How do you feel Laura?" Billy inquired. She looked up at her mother.

"Mommy?"

"Yes honey."

"My tummy doesn't hurt anymore."

The mother sobbed as she picked up her little angel. Billy, also in tears, stood up looking at his hands as he was opening and closing them slowly.

"What's wrong?" Will asked.

"My hands aren't hot, not even warm."

"Did something go wrong?" asked Taylor.

"I don't think so. It just felt different, a good kind of different."

"How do you feel?" asked her dad.

"I'm hungry." Her mom hugged her and cried.

"What's wrong, Mommy?"

"I'm just happy, darling."

Through teary eyes, Billy told the parents, "When y'all go back to the doctor for a check-up, I'd like to know what the results are. I hope they're positive."

"I don't know how we can thank you," the dad exclaimed.

"We don't know yet if anything has changed," Billy insisted"

"Something's changed," the mother proclaimed.

"I can see the sparkle in her eyes again."

Billy's dad, who had been extremely quiet until now, spoke.

"Only a mother would notice something like that."

"Can it be?" Will's mom questioned.

"Mom, if you feel instead of think," he stared at Billy and smiled, "you'd be surprised what you could do."

Billy and Will chuckled at the inside joke.

"Will, we need to toss some lines in. It's been a couple of weeks."

"You can say that again."

"You folks wanna come in for a cup of coffee or tea? I think my better half made some fresh lemonade earlier."

"No thanks, Mr. Roach. If you don't mind, the Mrs. here, and I, would like to carry our daughter in for some tests. We're kind of anxious."

"Oh, I understand. Coach, you and yours wanna try some lemonade and bundt cake. That would give us a short break from the farm chores."

"Sounds fine. I think we've got a few minutes . . and a few questions."

"As if I'm surprised...lemme go tell Joyce. Oh, good luck with your daughter's tests. I hope everything turns out alright." Bill shakes their hands.

"Thank you so much. You've been kind." They both hugged Billy. He kneels down again.

"Laura, sweetie, you come back and see me anytime, okay?"

"I will." she smiled with a glow.

"Next time you come back, I'll see if I can saddle up the miniature pony and carry you on a ride. Does that sound ok?"

"Oh yes, I like ponies. I have a Pretty Pony at home."

"You do?"

"Uh huh. I have to brush her hair a lot."

"Mommy and Daddy are ready to leave. I hope you're gonna be okay, kiddo."

"Oh yes, I don't like my stomach to hurt."

"Well, hopefully it won't ever hurt again. I'll see you later, alright?"

She hugged him, almost knocking her cap off.

"Okay."

"Thanks again." Mother repeated.

"Like I said, I don't know if it worked. I know it does on animals."

"We'll let you know as soon as we can." Father stated.

"I'd like that. Bye-now, good journey."

"Bye, thanks again." Mother said with tears in her eyes.

"Y'all be careful." Billy waved.

"Will do." He waved.

The years passed by with word in the wind that a young man was able to heal animals, and people. The news, surprisingly enough, spread slower than winter molasses. The family asked for their privacy as much as they could. Since the only 'patients' that this farm boy could heal had to be terminally ill, little was understood. Now, at the age of thirty-five, Billy and his family were getting about four to seven visitors a month. One day he and his father were repairing the barn's tin roof when Fate changed the family and community forever.

Billy and his dad didn't know the boards on the edge of the roof under the tin were rotted out. It collapsed under Billy's weight. He crashed to the ground, hitting his head on a rock slab.

"Son?!" Bill scrambled to the edge and peered over and saw his son's lifeless body lying on the ground.

"Joyce!"

He rushed toward the ladder as his wife came around the side of the house where she was working.

"Yes?"

"Billy fell off the roof. He's not moving."

"Oh, Lord!" She ran toward her men as Bill was coming down the ladder. He was stirring a little as his parents were coming around the side of the barn. He sat up just as they reached him.

"What happened?"

"The roof collapsed on you. Son, are you okay?" He was holding his head with both hands and spoke slowly.

"My head hurts. Owww!"

He pulled his hands from his head and saw blood on his palm. A lump the size of a 50 cent piece appeared above his right ear.

"Mmm, mmm, oh, that hurts."

"Are you okay?" It was Mother's turn to ask.

"I guess."

"You didn't hurt the rock, did you?"

"Oh, Daaad. Dad? Mom?"

"We're here, sweetie. You've got a shiner. I'll fix you an ice pack." He looked at them with a puzzled look in his eyes.

"You're my mother and father."

"Well, he's still got his memory." Dad joked.

"Yes, I remember. You're my parents. Yeah, I remember everything now." His voice faded in and out.

"Why don't we take a break now and let your mom put some ice on that." They helped him up and the three walked toward the house. Bill went to the bathroom. Mom washed her hands in the kitchen sink while Billy sat at the table. She gave him a wet cloth while she fixed the ice pack.

"Here, this ice should help the . . . Oh Lord!"
Bill walked in the room.

"What's wrong now?"
She turned her head and looked at her husband.

"There's no swelling. All the blood's gone, too."
Billy opened his eyes and smiled as he took a deep breath.

"It's okay, Mom. I understand now."

"Understand what? That you can heal yourself now?"

"Something like that." He smiled a peaceful smile that his parents had never seen in him before.
Bill said, "Let's eat lunch. If you feel up to it, we'll hit another lick after a bite to eat."
With that smile still on his face, he replied, "Sounds just fine."
After lunch the family walked back out to finish what they were doing.

"You two be careful on that roof."

"Your son's the one diving off on his head."

"Guess that roof was more rotten than we thought."
Billy followed.
As soon as Billy stepped out of the house, two sparrows flew down and landed on his right shoulder and head.

"That hasn't happened to you in a while, has it?"

"Yeah. Just, not around people and KJ.
(King Jr., after his father). Don't poop on my head, little one."
The delicate winged creature sat on the back of his head, chirped several times then flew up into the trees.

"Son, why do they do that?"

"There's no fear in me for them to feel. They know I'm a different creature than they are. They just see me as a part of nature."

"Smart, huh?"

"They're geniuses compared to you and me."

"Geniuses, huh?"

"Sure. They can build a house that won't blow down in the highest winds and never use a hammer, nails or glue to build it with. Pretty impressive, huh?"

"That just makes them master home builders." Dad exclaimed.

"Ah, but they don't build weapons of any kind, nor do they start wars."

"How can they? They're just animals."

"Have you seen the movie *The Birds*?"

"Point taken. Let's climb up and finish what we started."

"I'm ready," Billy chuckled. "We need to fix what I broke first, don't we?"

"Yeah, it wouldn't hurt."

The roof repairs took the rest of the day, after that were the usual chores. That night, while Billy and King were at their fishing hole, his parents were in deep discussion over their son's head banging experience. Joyce was telling her husband,

"I saw it. He was bleeding when he stepped through the door. By the time I got the ice crushed and wrapped in a towel . . . I mean it couldn't have taken me two or three minutes."

"I know, I was there. I was the one that suggested we don't shoot the mule just because he threw a shoe."

"Bill, I'm serious."

"Well what do ya want me to say? You know he's got a gift. We still don't know its limitations."

"Well, there was no limitation to that miracle." Mother proclaimed.

In the following weeks, the animals on the farm were acting strange, a good kind of strange. Every time Billy walked by a pen or pasture, the animals would come to greet him as if he were carrying a bucket of food. It went off and on for about a month, and then abruptly stopped.

A couple of years passed by when one Friday evening after chores, Billy and his father came inside and Joyce uttered,

"They say it's gonna be a meteor shower tonight. Do y'all wanna watch?"

"Definitely!" Billy was fast to answer.

"Yeah, I guess." Bill hesitated

"Well, don't sound overly enthused." Joyce grinned.

"I'll feel better after a shower."

"So will we." She picked.

"You go, Mom." Billy laughed.

The family, with KJ, sat outside in lawn chairs and watched the largest light show in the world. They were shooting from every direction. Billy sat on the grass with his new best buddy, KJ.

"I'm glad we let King breed the Hiles' female. I can see so much of his daddy in him."

"He turned out alright."

"I wish he'd quit layin' around my shrubs."

"You keep the critters out, don't cha, boy?" Billy smiled rubbing his old friend's belly.

Everyone watched in wonder as the universe worked her magic. About nine o'clock the 'older generation' went inside. Since star gazing was a part of fishing, Billy and KJ were not about to miss out. They relaxed on the grass side by side.

"Buddy, I'm really glad I got to know you. You and your dad have been a real blessing to me."

He scruffed his friend's neck while he spoke.

"You've both made great fishing pals."

He leaned over and hugged his big hairy friend.

"I'm sure glad we met."

An hour later Billy started dozing.

"Whoa, I gotta go to bed, buddy."

Just before he stepped in the door he turned, pointing his finger, and said, "KJ, stay outta mom's bushes before she puts a knot on your head. Good night, boy."

A quick shower and the day was over.

It was 1:23 am. The family was awakened by KJ's constant barking. The horses were also making a fuss about something. Then suddenly the nightlights flashed off and on, off and on.

"What was that?" Joyce asked.

"Probably some back roads lead foot hit a pole." Bill mumbled as he dangled his legs off the bed.

A dark shadow appeared at their bedroom door.

"Mom, Dad, get dressed."

"Son . . .?"

"Just get dressed, we've gotta go outside."

"Billy, if I get dressed at one thirty in the morning and it's not important . . ."

"Maybe it's another meteor." Their son spoke softly.

"Oh Lord, don't say that," Joyce said as she was getting dressed, "we'll have a hundred people at our doorstep again. You don't think one of the animals is out, do ya?"

"I hope not. Where're my shoes?" Bill fumbled around in the dark.

"They're in the kitchen next to the laundry room." As they both made their way through the home in the dark, Bill commented, "Sounds like it got quiet outside."

"You don't think something's wrong, do ya?"

"We'll know when we get there. Besides, Billy would've been back in by now if something was wrong. You ready, hun? Here's the light he set out for us."

As the couple went out to find their son, Mother was the first to speak.

"Bill?"

"What?" he answered.

"Listen."

"I ain't hearing anything."

"I know. There's no sound . . . no crickets, frogs, or night birds."

"Billy!" Joyce yelled.

"I'm over here." He was standing just on the other side of the fence in the field next to the house. He had his light off and was staring at an open field in the direction of the meteor crash site.

"Son, what are you doing?"

"What did we have to get dressed for?" Mother asked. Standing three feet away and still staring into an empty field, he answered, "We're here for them." His father started to ask, "Who are . . . Holy . . ."

Lights appeared, then a shape.

"Bill!" Joyce drew close to her husband. "Billy, be careful." Motherhood was in gear.

"Mom," he returned to his parents, smiling. "Dad, they're here for me."

"What? No, you can't go."

"Mom, I have to. I've overstayed my welcome."

"What're you talking about, Son?"

"The physical Billy you gave birth to, died."

"What? I don't understand . . . you mean you're not our son?"

"Oh, but I am. I have all his memories, fears, joys and pain. I'm more like a perfect clone, right down to the cellular state and Soul."

"But how? Why?"

"Do you remember the meteor crash?"

"You know we do," his father reiterated.

"Well, it wasn't exactly a meteor that crashed. It was a kind of shuttle craft like you see on *Star Trek*. I saw the craft crash. I helped free two people from the crash and was killed when a panel blew and hit me in the head. They regenerated my body in a matter of minutes using healthy tissue samples. They did a memory transfer, and then I was born again, so to speak. I was sent to live out a life to make up for the one that was lost. Now, they've come to take me home. I actually lived seven years longer than I was supposed to."

"Why?" his mother asked.

"I would have died from the same thing Uncle West and Granddad's uncle died of . . . Lou Gehrig's disease."

"How come you didn't die?"

"All my genes were run through a bio-filter. That's why I never got sick after the crash. These people are much, much more advanced than anything in this solar system."

"Who are they?" mom asked.

"They're explorers like Jacques Cousteau. Only they explore a dark, cold sea of stars. They look quite a bit like us. They call themselves Pleadians. Their planet hasn't seen a war in over seven centuries."

"Have you always known this?"

"No, Dad. I didn't know until I fell off the barn and hit my head. You could say it knocked some sense into me."

"What will you do now? What will happen to us? What…."

"Mom, slow down, first thing's first. In the morning you will find me deceased in bed. I will have died of an aneurism. I will join my friends on their journey."

A door opened from a portal of light.

"Son, how can tha . . . can they do all that?"

Billy smiled and walked close to the fence where his parents were standing in awe. He reached across to open the gate between the field and the yard.

"Dad, they live almost 10,000 light years from here and can travel the distance in less than twenty minutes. I think they can do anything imaginable."

"That's impossible." Bill exclaimed.

"So is the ability to heal. Besides, their ships are designed to travel at the speed of thought. If you understood wormholes...well...we won't get into all that. I know it works, but I don't know how to explain it. I have learned so much about them over the past three weeks. More and more information about them keeps coming to me and I don't exactly know how."

"Will you come back and visit?"

"I . . . don't really know. It's very possible."

"Won't you need a bag or clothes or . . ."

"Mom, I'll be just fine. It is I that should worry for you."
He hugged his mother for probably the last time.

"Dad?" He then hugged his father.

"Why tonight?" Bill asked his son.

"The meteor shower helped mask their entrance, and exit.
They think of everything!"
A male figure emerged from the column of light and walked
slowly toward the three at the gate.

"Wow, they do look a lot like us," Joyce quietly
commented.
The man approached, smiling with eyes of universal wisdom.
He was dressed in a silver outfit suited for space travel.

"Billy, I believe." They shook hands.

"You're Cleyton . . . aren't you?"

"Very good," the man smiled kindheartedly.

"How do I know your name?"

"There is a lot that will have to be explained to you,
but later. This is your mother and father?"

"Yes."

"Hi, I'm Bill."

"And... I'm Joyce."

"You have done a wonderful job raising him. I see his
spirit is well."

"We're gonna miss him."

"He will not be as far away as you think."

"You mean I can come back and visit?"

"Yes, but not anytime you want. We are doing tests in
this particular solar system, so we will be in and out of
this region."

"Then, you are scientists?" Bill felt the itch of curiosity.

"Yes. In fact, we are all scientists. We figured out how
to make our physical existence here a little easier to live with."

The three listened while the stranger spoke. He told of how the different parts of this universe are more progressed than others.

"This universe?" Joyce asked with barely hidden curiosity.

"Yes," smiling, "there are many universes. There are portals that allow ships to pass through and end up a hundred thousand light years away at a pre-designated point.
There are planets that are just entering the Stone Age and some that are inhabited by beings of great power that can travel from solar system to solar system without ever leaving their own home."

"That's impossible!" Bill exclaimed once again.

"Everyone in the universe is not like you, no one is. When you learn how to use the power of your nonphysical being you call the Soul, nothing is impossible.
I believe your son has shown you a small sample of this ability." Cleyton smiled with a prideful intelligence.

"Point taken," Bill agreed.

"Well, Billy, it is time for us to leave."

"Mom, Dad, I'll see you sometime in the future." His mother began to sob.

"Won't you need anything, a sweater, or . . ."

"He will not need anything. Ah!" He halted with his left index finger in the air. "You could bring your animal journal."

"Yeah, I could . . how did you know about that?"

"That will take some time to explain. It is safe to say, for now, that we know all about you and all of your possibilities in life."

"I'll take your word for it. Let me get my journal." He jogged back into the house while his parents and his new guide spoke amongst themselves.

"Your son will be just fine. We will put him through studies that will open his mind and Soul to new horizons." He talked until the house doors slammed shut, signaling Billy's imminent return.

"It sounds like he'll be in good hands." Bill stated.

"I'm just gonna miss him," Joyce's eyes were filled with tears.

"Here it is." Billy was as excited as a schoolboy again. He fondly gazed upon his parents and KJ once more, after the old dog realized the invisible craft wasn't a danger.

"I can't call or write, but if you're out at night and you see a shooting star, wave hi, 'cause it might be me!"
He hugged his parents and smiled for the last time. They watched as the two disappeared in a beam of light. The craft left their planet in the blink of an eye. There was no sound as it rose from the field, traveling at the speed of light. Not so much as a blade of grass moved. The couple fell to the ground and stared at the night sky. KJ sat down with them as they examined the universe, noticing a little more beauty and knowledge than it ever had before.

The End...for now

School Spirit

One beautiful morning an attractive young woman wearing
shorts, tank top, and headphones jogs down a semi-rural,
suburban street. She notices something move out of the corner
of her eye, like everyone does occasionally. She glances to her
right to satisfy her curiosity and sees nothing but an open field.
She slows her jogging to a stop. 'An open field?' she thinks,
'That's impossible, an empty field where the town school is
supposed to be?' The school was gone, everything and everyone
was gone. . no building, no ball field, no parking lot, electrical or
phone lines. Taking her headphones off, she stares with
skepticism. A car skids upon the sidewalk and nudges the phone
pole. The jogger hardly notices the careless driver's incident.
A man gets out, and he too, stares at the empty field. He, almost
mesmerized, takes his cell phone out, and starts dialing.
"Get me the police . . . or . . . or somebody." His voice is quiet
and unsure. The woman walks over to his slightly damaged car.
"Where is it?" She asks.
"I dunno." He replies.
They both fall silent until a sheriff's deputy arrives a few minutes
later.
    Officer Dave Tender, a six-year veteran of the Lotus County
Sheriff's Department, responds to the call.
"Have a lil' accident, huh?" he says jokingly, noticing no one
was hurt.
The man and woman turn and stare at the deputy.
"What's wrong?" He asks. The smile disappears from his face
as the three slowly turn and stare at the vacant field.
"Holy Jesus," he whispers softly. He's on the radio in a matter
of seconds.
"HQ, this is Dave!"
"Go ahead, Dave."
"Tara, I need you to get the sheriff out here to the high school
immediately!"

"Why, what'cha got?"

"You wouldn't believe me if I told ya. Just send 'im out here, now." His voice fades in shock.

"You got it hun. Headquarters out."

Meanwhile, across town on a disturbing the peace call, Sheriff Marc Fergus discusses the matter at hand with two elderly brothers, seventy-year-old Dale Yates and his sixty-eight-year-old brother Chris.

"I don't care what you are arguing about this month. I just want it stopped. The high school is having its homecoming this week, and I'm gonna have my hands full. So I'm not gonna have time to be a referee for you again. So, whatever you guys…"

"Headquarters to Sheriff…"

"S'cuse me a second fellas. Go ahead Tara."

"Sheriff, somethin's going on out at the high school."

"Why? What's wrong?"

"Dave didn't say. He just sounded a little shook up."

Breathing a heavy sigh he answers, "Well, tell 'im I'm on my way. Sheriff out."

Turning back to the brothers, he asks, "You guys can behave the rest of the day, can't cha?"

"We'll be good, Sheriff," the eldest brother replies.

"We'll talk later," he remarks as he opens the car door. After climbing in his unit, he grabs his mike.

"Sheriff to Dave . . . Dave, you there?"

"Go ahead, Sheriff."

"What's going on out at the school?"

"Sheriff, you're not gonna believe this. It's the school . .well . . . it's the everything!"

Chuckling, he answers, "My number one deputy hasn't been gettin' into ol' man Jenkins' special spring water this morning, has he?"

"God Almighty, you gotta see this Sheriff!"

"Well, what is it already?"

"Just get here as quick as you can."

B

"I'll be there in five. Keep your shirt on."

Three and a half minutes later the sheriff arrives to a gathering crowd around the deputy's squad car. As he gets out, he moans "Holy . . ."

"You see what I mean!" the deputy blurts. "I don't know what to think, Sheriff. I've never seen anything like it. Hell, I've never even heard of anything like it."

"Just take it easy."

"Well, what are we gonna do?"

"Call Scully and Mulder."

"Huh?"

"Never mind," remarks the Sheriff, as he stands in disbelief. "Try to keep everyone as calm as you can. I gotta make a call." Walking over to his unit, he reaches inside, grabs the mike, and radios back to dispatch.

"Tara, it's me."

"This is base. Hey, what's goin' on out at the high school? We've gotten a half dozen prank phone calls here sayin' that the school's missin'. Sounds like someone's tapped the water supply," she chuckles.

"Look, Tara," the sheriff states firmly, "I need you to get a hold of Federal Agent Dan Speller in Knoxville. Do you remember him?"

"Yeah," she answers. "He helped with the Stover kidnapping case several years ago."

Brian Stover, age six at the time, was illegally abducted by his father during a custody battle in the small town of Mt. Juliet. Sheriff Fergus and Special Agent Speller worked well together to solve the case and got the young boy back home safely.

"Yeah, that's right. Tell him I need him here ASAP!"

"You're not gonna tell me that the school is really missin'?"

"Look, Tara, I don't have time right now. Just get him here as quick as you can. It's startin' to get a little crowded around here."

"I'm on it. I'll contact him for ya."

"Thank ya, darlin'. Sheriff out."

C

As the crowd keeps growing, the sheriff tries to speak over the noisy mob.

"Look folks, take it easy. We'll figure this out somehow."

"Where's our children?" cries one woman.

"Where's the school?" cries another.

"Where's my wife?"

"Where's my husband?"

"Sheriff, this is gettin' outta hand." The young deputy was getting nervous.

"Yeah, I know." The sheriff replies,

"Call everyone on duty, and I mean everyone. Tell 'em a Code Blue is in effect until I say otherwise."

Dave walks over to his unit and starts making calls of his own.

"Tara, you there?"

"I can barely hear you Dave, but go ahead."

He climbs in the car and rolls up the window to quiet the noise of the crowd.

"Tara, we need you to call Bud, Jake, and Joanna. Tell 'em to get uniformed and get out here to our location, A-S-A-P. How copy, over."

"I read you loud an' clear. Dave, is the thing really missing?"

"Tara, listen to me. We are in Code Blue, I say again...Code Blue...sheriff's orders. How copy, over? (Code Blue is radio lingo for, 'All officers are to be on duty or on standby and keeping silent about the emergency at hand'.) Sheriff Fergus and all but one of his officers have had some military training. Many people in the county have either CB radios or police scanners so the Force kept as much talk as they could off the air.

"Yeah, yeah, I heard ya. I know what a Code Blue is. Ya'll betta' not be pullin' my leg. How can it just disappear? "

"We're clueless. It's the blamedest thing I've ever seen. There's nothin' here I tell ya. I mean nothin'. We're tryin' to figure this out ourselves right at the moment. The only thing we know at this point is that the crowd here is gettin' larger by the minute and we need reinforcements."

D

"Well, I do know that Bud is out fishin' in Mill Creek. I'll try calling him and then everyone else." The dispatcher acknowledged. "Good. Call Pam and Lil' Eddie too. We can swear 'em back in as temps. We need all the help we can get right now."
Signing off, the deputy dreaded the task to come. He steps back into the crowd and tries to get a word in with the sheriff. "We've got reinforcements on the way!" He yells over the crowd of about sixty very bewildered people.
"Good! We need to tape the place off!" He said loudly. "First make out a report and get our sidewalk jumper's car outta here!"
"Sheriff, we don't have that much tape!" The deputy remarks as he points across the vacant fifteen-acre field.
"I've got more at the station! I'll have Joanna bring some out! She just called me!"

While the sheriff laid out what little plan he had come up with, the town's newspaper sent out a reporter to investigate the first real, supernatural phenomenon in Lotus County, Tennessee.

The paper, *The Mt. Juliet Print*, is fairly small, with only twenty-three employees, which includes the distributors. It was left to Penny Shepherd by her parents, Meryl and John, after they retired some ten years earlier. "No news is bad news," her father used to tell her as a child. Besides, the biggest thing that ever happened around this three-thousand-person town in a while was one of the town drunks setting fire to city hall's dumpster. And he didn't do that on purpose. Lit cigars and moonshine have never mixed well together.

However, on this day, there is news that this family paper has never seen or heard of before. The reporter, Nathan Powell, got his job at *The Mt. Juliet Print* right out of high school. He never thought when he graduated four years ago that he would be doing a story on the disappearance of his alma mater.
"Sheriff?"
"Please, Nathan, not now."
"Sheriff, you know we have to print something about this."
"Yeah, I know, but I'm up to here, (slicing his right hand across his throat), in worried parents, husbands, and wives."

E

"But I've got a job to do," pushing the way most reporters do. "Look Nathan, I don't know what 'n tarnation is goin' on yet myself, so I can't tell ya a thing. You know as much as I do." Turning back toward the crowd, he yells. "Folks, take it easy! Please stay back until we know more about what's goin' on!"

Ten to fifteen minutes later officer Joanna Seese pulls up. Moments later, deputies Bud Polk and Jake Deery come driving in. The crowd noise dies down slightly at the sight of new deputies driving up. Joanna is the first to reach the sheriff. She looks into the vacant field with a very wide-eyed look on her face. With an empty feeling inside, she forces the words through her lips. "Sheriff...?"

"I know Jo. I don't have the words either." He left the crowd to meet with his deputies.

"Jake, see if you can keep everyone back. We don't know what dangers are here."

"Everyone?" Jake looks over the large crowd, then back at the sheriff with a smirky smile.

"Just do the best you can, without hurting anyone." The sheriff smirks back.

"OK, y'all step back. You heard the sheriff."

"What're we gonna do? Where's our families?" one frantic woman asks.

"Just stay back, please!" the big man insists.

"Bud," the sheriff continues, "you and Jo tape off the entire school area."

"The entire area?" Bud asks.

"Yes deputy, the entire school grounds. Stay ten feet out of the perimeter until we know what's goin' on here."

"You da' boss."

"Oh, Bud, when you're through, stay on the far side, on the side of the fence row to keep anyone from crossing the line."

"I'm headed that way right now" Bud responds as he grabs the police tape and heads to his destination.

           *   *   *

It's lunchtime now. It has been at least three hours since this ordeal first began. The closest TV station had gotten word of what had happened in this "one-horse town" and had dispatched one of their news crews to view and confirm the rumored story. "Sheriff," big Jake summoned while pointing toward the news van. "We've got company!"
"Oh, great." the sheriff dreads aloud.
"Sheriff," from the radio.
"Now what? . . . Go ahead, Tara."
"Sheriff, your Alpha Sierra is ten mikes away from town. He called and I told him to go straight to your location. How copy, over?"
"Best and only good news I've gotten today. Thanks, Tara. Oh Tara, one more thing...Give me one hotel with Alpha Sierra before contacting Golf." (Radio lingo for: Give me 1 hour with Agent Speller before contacting the Governor's office). "How copy over?"
"I'll start your time in twenty mikes, over?"
"Can you give me thirty?"
"I'll give ya forty if you want it."
"You know you're an angel, don't cha."
"Yeah, I know. That's why I make the big bucks. Oh, Dave said you wanted a cupla' more deputies?"
"I could sure use 'em."
"Lil' Eddie and Pam are on their way. How's that sound?"
"Excellent. We'll be here. It's not like we're goin' anywhere. Sheriff out."

At this point, the news crew starts setting up as the crowd grows up to around 200 spectators of onlookers and worried families and friends. The entire county police force felt like they were fighting a war all by themselves. All of a sudden, a stranger, with very short salt and pepper hair, dressed in peach, Chinese clothing and sandals, appears at the far end of the mob.

With a happy, glowing smile on his face, he asks a woman in the crowd, "What seems to be the problem?"

With tears in her eyes and a quiver in her voice she replies, "Our school is gone . . . it, it's just vanished."

"No, it is still there."

"NO?!" She insists, in panic. "You're not from here . . . our families are gone!" She frantically waves her arms and hands as she speaks.

"They are still here. You just cannot see them," he replies calmly, still smiling.

He stands there for a few moments with his eyes closed and hands tucked under opposite sleeves. He opens his eyes, turns his head, and looks deeply into the woman's eyes.

In the most serene voice she had ever heard, he calmly replies, "Everything will be just fine."

He then turns and steps across the police line and walks ten feet into the perimeter. All of time seems to come to a standstill as the now, not so hysterical woman watches in awe.

The stranger sits down in a cross-legged position on the ground. Another person asks her, "What's he doin'?" She shrugs her shoulders in an 'I don't know' fashion without saying a word.

In what seems like only a few seconds, the stranger's entire physical being begins to flash like a florescent light trying to turn on, and off. This caught the eye of about ten to fifteen people who begin to first gasp, then mumble, and finally a scream as the man disappears.

"He's gone!" one of the men yells. "Did you see that? He just vanished!"

The commotion caught the attention of a few of the deputies including the sheriff, who was otherwise distracted by the media and the rest of the crowd. Officer Polk, who had seen something out of the corner of his eye, walked through the crowd to investigate.

"He disappeared, too!" one woman yells.

H

"No one disappeared. Now stay the hell back! Sheriff!"
The impatient deputy radios from the far side of the field.
"What 'cha got, Bud?" he answers as he looks towards his end
of the field.
"The crowd here is gettin' stupid."
"Watch your radio mouth, deputy. You're an officer of the law."
"Yes sir."

Back at the Pruitt household, Annah is outside singing to
herself while weeding her flowerbed. In the distance, she hears
the sounds of sirens. Two to three minutes later, more sirens are
heard. 'Someone's got problems,' she thinks. The phone rings.
She takes off her gloves and steps inside the kitchen door.
"Hello?"
"Annah!" Maria's mother Juanita was hysterical.
"Turn on the news quickly!"
"Why?" She asks walking to the remote.

A female newscaster is shooting live from the school scene.
*". . not yet. We're still trying to get some more information at
this time from the county sheriff who is in charge. No sign
whatsoever of the school or its occupants. It's as if it was . .
never here. As you can see behind us, there is nothing but an
open field with several sheriff's deputies taping off the area. If
this is some kind of hoax Jim, then the whole town is in on it.
And, by the reactions of the crowd here, something very strange
is going on . . ."*
"Oh Lord, not my baby! This has gotta be a joke." Annah
succumbs to the news.
"Annah? . . . Annah!"
"Juanita, what're we gonna do?"
"Carlos iz on his way home. We're coming by to get chu."
*"Sources say the school has been missing since about 8:30 or
9:00 this morning...."*
"Please hurry!"
"We're in this together . . . We'll be okay."

I

"I'll be ready before you get here. This is impossible. Schools don't just disappear!"

"I know. I don't know what to think."

"... *more on this story as it unfolds. This is Hope McKenzie ... Channel 2 News ... back to you, Jim.*"

"*Thanks, Hope. We'll keep you in touch more as this story develops.*"

As the news cast signs off, a large crowd of people could be seen. Some were crying and screaming while others hold up signs that read "The End is Near" and "John 12:31."

*   *   *

"Mom, where's my blue skirt?" Janie Pruitt yelled to her mother as she was getting ready for school. "Never mind, I found it."

The Ready Mixed radio station was throwing out tunes from the Fifties all the way to the present time. ♪ '*Devil with the Blue Dress, blue dress on, devil with the blue dress on.*' ♪ Janie, seventeen, smiles a naughty smile as she holds up her blue skirt in front of the mirror. It has been just her and her mother since her father passed away when she was eight. He died in a plant accident saving a fellow worker's life.

This is the story the family got. In the shipping warehouse where he was working, a half-ton crate snapped a bolt in the shelf it was sitting on and slid down. Before it made the ten-foot drop to the concrete floor, Janie's father, Erick pushed Carlos out of harm's way. Erick died three days later at St. Mary's Memorial Hospital. The plant insurance took care of Annah and Janie's needs.They also set up a memorial in Erick's name and financed Janie's future college plans. Carlos, his wife Juanita, and their now seventeen year old daughter Maria, have been very good friends with Janie and her mother Annah ever since.

Carlos has always felt an obliging love toward his family's new found friends. Picnics, grill-outs, and holiday events were part of the two families' togetherness. Over the years, Maria and Janie grew up together as best friends and were almost inseparable. In both households, the conversations about Janie always involved Maria, and vice versa. The two friends took turns driving to school. It was Maria's turn this morning.

Janie was almost ready when she got there at 7:30 sharp. Maria went in to see Annah Madre, as she called her, while she waited on Janie.

"Are you girls ready for the big game tonight?" Annah always checked on their school functions.

"Yes, ma'am. We're havin' a pep rally today. They think they're gonna rally us up for the big homecoming game tonight," she said nostalgically.

"Oh? And for some reason you think they won't."

"They can't!" she replies wide-eyed and smiling. "Everybody is already to the max about this game!"

"Oh, I'll just stay out of your way, then." Annah Madre always had a good sense of humor.

"Let's go. Bye, Mom." Janie was ready.

"Oh, Janie, not your blue skirt."

"Mo-oom."

"I know, I know. You girls be careful."

"Bye, Annah Madre."

"Bye, Mom."

"Bye. Have fun at school today, but not . . too much fun," she said, slowly pointing to her daughter in her short attention-gettin' skirt. With "Gold Dust Woman" by Fleetwood Mac coming out of the car stereo, the two sped off to school.

The ninth through the twelfth grade students were piling into the building while the JRROTC students were raising the American and Tennessee flags. By the time the bell rang, everyone was in his or her appointed room, except for the usual stragglers.

The principal, Randall Glausto, usually a stick in the mud, was playing rock and pop music over the school's loudspeaker.

K

♪ *Please allow me to introduce myself. I'm a man of wealth and fame'* . . . ♪

At fifty-nine years of age, and very set in his ways, even he was fired up for this homecoming B-ball game. Now he's doing the Rolling Stones. He wants this game baaad.

Ms. Desiree Evans, the forty-looks-thirty psychology teacher, is the most well liked teacher in the school. This very attractive psych major has a degree in Eastern Philosophy that she uses to freely instruct students, teachers, and their families in the art of meditation in the gym twice a month. She studied in Nepal for eighteen months outside a Buddhist temple in Katmandu. Apparently, Ms. Evans is the one responsible for the choice of music coming out of the PA system. Principal Glausto told her to 'bring in some music that the students will like and put it on the loud speaker.'

"I heard Ms. Evans is the school DJ today," Janie whispered to Maria.

"Yeah? I heard Principal Glausto was gonna bring in some Beach Boys and Perry Como records." Both girls giggle.

"Listen up, class!" Their homeroom teacher began. "Today's pep rally will be at 8:30 after homeroom. So, go straight to the gym after the bell, and don't dilly dally. Keep working on your homecoming posters if you haven't finished yet. They will be judged right after lunch."

While homeroom was taking care of its business, the school custodian, Moses Trent, was busy in the gym cleaning and singing. ♫ *"Mt. Juliet rolls... on do-own the road."*♪ Mr. Moses, a black man in his late seventies, is very highly respected in the school, and the community. He could fix anything short of a computer or a nuclear reactor. Everyone in and around town says that he is the one man that has been keeping the school together for the past thirty-six years. If it was broke, he could fix it. He knew every square inch of the facility and grounds. The school was built in 1944. It has been remodeled and added on to twice since it was first constructed. Moses, whose grandfather was a sharecropper, was there through it all, the building and the remodeling.

L

While he was in one part of the school singing his school spirit
worksong, the cafeteria workers were singing and chanting their
way through the morning as well.

"We're gonna beat those Livingston Blue Devils this year. I can
feel it!" Ms. Edna Pickard had the entire cafeteria staff thumpin'
and bakin'.

"Go, girl!" Mrs. Wilkerson egged her on. It would seem that the
whole school was being pumped up for this game.

When it came time for the pep rally, everyone piled into the
gym. While filing in, the Social Studies teacher Mrs. Ambra
Bennett pulls Ms. Evans aside and asks, "Can you cover for me
for about fifteen minutes after the rally? I've gotta pick up a
couple of things from the Dollar General. School supply doesn't
have 'em."

"Sure, hun," she answers with her award-winning brown-eyed
smile. "I've gotta get a few things from the office first, but I'll
be there."

"Thanks. I won't be long."

Right after the pep rally, Mrs. Bennett goes to the parking lot
and gets in her car. Just as she is leaving, faster than the blink
of an eye, she drives out of one side of the parking lot and comes
right back in the other.

"My God!" she gasps as the brakes were slammed. SCREECH!
Unable to complete a thought, she sits behind the wheel panting
and shaking as if she had just seen a ghost. "That's impossible,"
she says to herself while holding her foot on the brake. She then
proceeds slowly out of the parking lot once more. Again, she
drives out and immediately reappears on the other side. "God!"
she yells, putting her car in park. With the engine still running,
she gets out very quickly and runs into the school. Ms. Evans is
walking out of the office when she bumps into the hysterical
history teacher.

"You gotta see this! You gotta see this!"

Principal Glausto hears the commotion from his office and
comes out.

"Principal, you gotta see this!"

M

"Ms. Desiree, what's going on?"

"I don't know. It's something we gotta see," smiling to ease the tension.

"Come on! Come on!" Mrs. Bennett is frantic as she leads them out the door.

"What're you doing?" The principal insists.

"Just watch!" she demands.

She gets back into her little Saturn that is still idling in park, and proceeds as she had done twice before. When her car disappears at one entrance and reappears in the other, the principal, for the first time in his life, is speechless. Ms. Desiree stood there, wide-eyed, with her mouth awkwardly hanging open.

"There!" shrieks Mrs. Bennett. "You see what I mean?!"

"That's impossible," the principal mutters.

"That's what I said!"

Glausto turned to the psychology teacher. "Ms. Desiree?"

"I don't know what to think," she says.

"You studied with those Monks, didn't you?" He was referring to her time in Nepal.

"Well, they didn't tell me everything." She pauses for a few seconds. "I have an idea." Walking to the edge of the parking lot, she picks up a rock.

"What're you gonna do?" Glausto questions.

"Just watch." She says instinctively.

She walks to the edge of the lot where the car and driver disappeared and threw the rock. Everyone immediately turns to see it come bouncing across the other side.

"What does it mean?" questions the principal.

"It has the same energy of motion coming in as it does going out." Desiree softly speaks.

"Oh my God, we're stuck here!" Panic hits Mrs. Bennett.

"Don't get'n a wad," he says. "Ms. Evans?" The puzzled look on his face is holding a few questions.

"Well . . . it looks like we're in some kind of vortex."

I can't, I can't really explain it. We're still part of the town, but we're different nonetheless. Principal, what time have you got?"
"I've got . . . hmmm," he says, tapping his Timex. "My watch has stopped working."
He looks at the now calmer history teacher. "Mrs. Bennett, what time have you got?"
"Huh? Oh, I've got . . . mine's not working either."
"Ms. Evans, what's going on?"
"Principal, I think you might find that every watch, clock and time piece in the school has come to a complete stop."
"Why's that?"
"Because time doesn't really exist here, or it moves so slowly that we can't notice it."
"I don't understand any of this." He reiterates.
"Well, if it's any consolation, I'm feelin' pretty out of place myself." She politely remarks.
"Let's go back inside. We'll try to figure something out."
Both teachers follow him back into the school building. All three keep glancing over their shoulder as they walk inside. As they step through the doors, they found Moses staring in bewilderment. The trio stare back for a moment without uttering a word.
Glausto was the first to speak.
"Did you see . . .?"
"Yes sir, everything," he quickly responds.
"Moses, we need to keep this low profile until we have more information."
"Yes sir. I understand," recognizing the severity of the problem.
"The other teachers will need to know." Mrs. Bennett began.
"We don't even know how long this'll last."
"Agreed. Ms. Evans, make a school announcement and have all the teachers meet us in the cafete. . Who the. . who are you? What are you doing in my school?"
Everyone turns to see a stranger, dressed in peach-colored, Eastern-looking clothes, who has just stepped into the hallway.
"Can I help you?" asked the principal.

All eyes were on the smiling man.

"The question should be, May I help you?" The youthful glow from the man's face reveals many wrinkles from lots of smiling he had apparently done in his lifetime.

"Are you responsible for all this?" asks the suspicious principal.

"No, I am not, you are....you all are."

Staring into everyone's eyes, he waits for a response. His eyes glow with a wisdom like none of them had ever experienced.

"But how are we responsible? We don't even know what's going on!" The principal becomes a little agitated.

"Come, we will talk."

The stranger led them into the vacant classroom where he had appeared. "Sit, please," he tells them. After everyone was seated and once again focused on him, he begins to speak.

"First, allow me to introduce myself. My name is Bo Don See. You may call me Master Bo. My people have been training many, many years for events such as this."

"What's going on?" asks Mrs. Bennett.

"I am afraid that you are going to have more questions than I will have time to answer. You will need to leave this place as soon as possible. The longer you stay here, the harder it will be to return. You will soon lose your will to leave."

The principal was quiet almost two minutes, "But, where are we?"

"You have traveled into another dimension. Let me explain in a way that you will understand. Everything is energy." He smiles brightly. "This place that we are in now is the dimension just beyond the physical one. There are many, many levels of existence to life. The non-physical existence of a person or animal, the object you call the Soul, is the only real existence of life. It has untold power and capabilities that the human mind could not possibly understand. It has no beginning, middle, or end, as some of you have gotten to study," he said looking directly into Ms. Evans' beautiful brown eyes.

"How did you know?" She also smiles.

Chuckling, he responds, "The eyes are the windows to the soul. When the school, the entire school, was preparing for an event, for one exact moment the souls and minds here became synchronized, in unity, causing a cosmic flux in the time/space continuum, throwing the existence here off balance and pushing it into the next realm of existence."

"You mean we're not real anymore?" the headstrong principal questioned.

"No. As a matter of fact, you have never been more real."

"Has this sort of thing ever happened before?" asks Mrs. Bennett.

"Yes, probably more often than you think. Do you remember the Roanoke colony?"

"Of course. From 1585 to 1587, the entire Roanoke colony disappeared without a trace. I am the history teacher you know."

"Roanoke, the Mayan and Inca Indians are just several of many examples." The master continued. "I come from an age-old school that sends out guides such as myself to help get people and things back to their chosen places in the material world. You see, sometimes we as humans are so caught up in our own thoughts and actions that we do not consider the consequences of either. Consequences that are physical are easier to see and deal with. However, the consequences that you cannot see, hear, smell, touch, or taste are usually ignored until it is too late. This place we are in now is very different from the physical world. Time and space has little value here. Your mind only accepts what it has been conditioned to believe. That is why you do not understand what is going on. Too many of you have appeared here at once. You must return."

"But how?" Principal Glausto becomes convinced.

"Conscious thought got you here, and unconscious thought will get you back. We must put the entire school to sleep and shut down all conscious judgment. I will do the rest, with a little help," looking at the psychology teacher.

Q

"I'll help where I can," she glows.

"I know you will." He returns the smile. "First, let all of the teachers and staff know that we are going to have a little nap time. I will need this man," motioning toward Moses, "and I will need your chemistry teacher."

"Why? What're you gonna do?" Glausto curiously asks.

"We are going to emit a harmless sleeping agent through the ventilation system, at which time she and I will be in the office chanting a prayer of remembrance, so to speak, over the intercom."

"Very well then. I'll make the announcement that we're gonna have a quiet time. We'll need to get the cafeteria staff to sit at the lunch tables and make sure no one is having gym class either. Moses, you and Ms. Evans go with Mr., Master Bo, and take care of your end and I'll take care of mine."

"Wait!" Moses holds his hand up. "What's gonna happen to us when we get out of the twilight zone?"

"You will remember this and me only as déjà vu. You will return to the exact moment you left."

Everyone stops dead in their tracks and stares at the soft-spoken man of wisdom.

"Remember, the non-physical existence does not recognize our time and space. It is an illusion of the mind." The master reiterates.

"Damned if I understand it, but I'm willing to go along just to get outta here. The students would freak if they knew." Shaking his head, the principal is the first to walk out of the room.

Moses, Ms. Evans, and Master Bo walked down the hall to the chemistry classroom. Ms. Evans calls the teacher out into the hall. At that same time, the principal is making his on-the-fly announcement over the intercom:

"Attention, please. I need all teachers and staff to meet me in the cafeteria at this time. Give your students study time. This won't take but a minute. Thank you."

R

"Class," began Mr. Mastin, "open your books to chapter seven and go over your chemical compositions. Janie, you're in charge until I get back. Oh, and Jerry, stay away from the Bunsen Burners!" Jerry grins and the rest of the class laughed. The teacher steps into the hall and is suprised to see the salt-and-pepper haired stranger with Moses and Desiree.

"Troy, this is Master Bo. Master Bo, this is our chemistry teacher, Troy Mastin. The master bows to the teacher.

"We have a dilemma on our hands." She told him.

In just a few minutes while walking to the cafeteria, She lays out the plan and what is going on.

"You don't really expect me to believe all this?"

"Look at your watch," Moses says, shaking his head.

Tapping his watch, Mr. Mastin exclaims, "It's stopped."

"Every clock in the school has stopped, too," the custodian replies.

"But how . . .?"

"Look, we don't have much time." She pauses and looks the others. "Sorry, no pun intended."

"How are my chemicals gonna work in this, environment?"

"Those chemicals, as you call them," Master Bo explains, "have the exact same energy qualities in this existence as you and I do. However, they would not have the same effect on someone who is outside of this place."

"So what do we do?" Mr. Mastin asked.

"Like I said, you and Moses are gonna put the gas through the ventilation system, go back to your class, and have your students lay their heads down on their desks. Every student must be present and seated. Master Bo and I will do the rest."

"And you're sure this'll work?" The teacher worried.

"Yes," says the American Master, "It has before."

"How many times have you done this, Master Bo?"

"A few." His usual smile brightens. "Trust me." he answers as they walk toward the cafeteria.

"How many people know about this?"

"Just a handful," she claims.

"The fewer that know, the easier this will be." The master concluded.

"I can understand that." The chem. teacher agrees.

All of the school staff, cafeteria workers included, were seated while the principal spoke. "The whole school will take 15-20 minutes of silent time. The object of this will be to reflect on our purpose and schedule on the upcoming game. This mental exercise is a psychological experiment. I know it sounds a little strange, but I myself," trying to sound convincing, "have checked into this. I have found that being in the right state of mind, without distractions, makes any task easier. Besides, if it doesn't work, you can blame Ms. Evans, our psychology teacher!"

He was looking for a laugh, and got only a few chuckles.

"Everyone, including myself, is gonna lay their heads down on their desks, or tables in this case," opening his arms to the lunchroom tables. "The office staff here will go ahead and stand fast." Turning to the three that had just walked in, he asks, "Where's our visitor?"

"He's . . . using the restroom," Ms. Evans says slowly, knowing that he had in fact stayed out of sight so as not to raise any suspicions. "Oh, okay. The rest of you teachers can return to your classes, and make sure all of your students are accounted for and seated. The teachers file out, leaving behind the cafeteria staff, office workers, Principal Glausto, Ms. Evans, Moses, and Troy Mastin. The principal walks toward the cafeteria door to speak quietly with his motley trio.

"How soon will y'all be ready?" he asks nervously. "Mr. Mastin?"

"It will take me about 15 minutes." He assures him.

"I can be ready in 10." Moses answered.

Taking a deep breath, the principal exclaims, "Well, as the kids would say, let's rock. Ms. Evans, go tell Master Bo we're ready to get started."

"He's in the office waiting on me now."

T

"Well, don't keep 'im waitin'. Good luck, everyone. I'll see you on the other side." With all smiling slightly, they depart. "Ms. Evans," Moses begins, "If I shut off the ventilation going into the office like Master Bo asked, how will you two go to sleep?"

"I believe the Master will attend to that need."

"Do you think he can?"

"Yes Mr. Moses, not a doubt in my mind," patting him on his shoulder, she answered smiling from ear to ear.

A short time later, with the joint efforts of an expert custodian and a very intelligent chemist, the odorless fumes started filling the school's heating and air conditioning system. In the office, the Master nodded to Ms. Evans. "It is time." She got on the intercom and started the announcement.

"Ladies and gentlemen, boys and girls, please lay your heads down and relax." Her voice was soft and very soothing. "We're gonna put tests and troubles behind us at this moment. We're gonna put ourselves in a state of tranquility by wiping away all negative thoughts and start anew." This went on for about three or four minutes before she turns her head and sees Master Bo sitting in a cross-legged position on the floor. There is a serene look about him, as if he doesn't have a care in the world. Opening his eyes, he looks at her and motions for her to sit beside him.

"Are you sure we're gonna go back to the exact moment we left?" As he smiles back at her, a golden light starts to appear around his head and shoulders. She quietly sits down, feeling on the inside as if she were going downhill on a roller coaster. It was like nothing she had ever felt.

*   *   *

U

Sheriff Marc Fergus and Special Agent Dan Speller are trying to come up with some answers. The crowd in their vicinity numbered in the hundreds. The governor, with more money than common sense, finally dispatched a local National Guard unit to help with security and crowd control. There are seven news crews with cameras and lights everywhere. Nobody really knows how many choppers are in the air. However, one veteran soldier in the crowd was noted as saying, "They're thicker than the mosquitoes on the Ho Chi Minh."

"Look, Sheriff, we need to talk." Agent Speller spoke with a straight look on his face.

"All right." The sheriff nodded.

"Alone," he states more seriously.

"It's too crowded here." They could barely hear each other.

"Let's get in my unit. Jake, you and Dave keep a close eye on everything."

"Yes sir."

They climbed into the sheriff's car. There is a moment of silence before Sheriff Fergus spoke.

"It must be something important to need to shut everyone else out."

"Marc . . . what I'm about to tell you could cost me my job."

"Dan we've known each other almost four years. You obviously trust me or we wouldn't be sittin' here."

"I do. This isn't easy." Agent Speller takes a deep breath then continues speaking.

"Look, what I'm about to tell you goes against every department regulation in the Bureau. But, it might have some bearing on this case."

"You know something, don't you?"

"About seven years ago, the FBI got called on a case in Macon, Missouri. A family of four was reported missing. The mother and father didn't show up for work and the kids never reported for school. To make a long story short, the local PD called us in on suspicion. The home showed no sign of forced entry.

All the doors and windows were locked from the inside.
No struggle in the residence and both cars were still in the drive.
No jewelry or possessions were missing that we could tell.
They were all missing for two days before anyone reported it.
The strangest thing about it was . . . well . . ."
"Spit it out, Dan."
"Well, all the clocks in the house were stopped at the exact same
time, except for the stove,which was blinking 12:00, like there
was some sort of power surge or outage."
"What're you saying?"
"There were no power outages in or around the town at the time.
I'm saying the case was unsolved . . . We don't know what
happened to the family. They were never found. It was kept
hush-hush because of the media, alien abduction, the end of time,
that sort of thing. We didn't want a bunch of religious cult
fanatics swarming the town. They were just reported missing."
"And you think that has something to do with this case?
"I don't know."
"But this is an entire school, parking lot, cars, planted trees,
ball field."
"I know, it's on a grander scale. What I'm sayin' is . . . they
might not come back. So, just try to prepare yourself. I know
it's har . . . Holy God!"
Staring out the windshield of the police cruiser, they could see
the shadowy outline of the school flashing like a florescent light
trying to come on...and off. They get out and stare in disbelief.
All of a sudden, soldiers, helicopters, news crews, and spectators
start vanishing in the exact reverse order that they showed up.
Last to show up, first to vanish, then everyone was gone.

One beautiful morning, an attractive young woman wearing
shorts, tank top, and headphones jogs down a semi-rural,suburban
street. She notices something move out of the corner of her eye,
like everyone does occasionally.

W

She glances to her right to satisfy her curiosity and sees nothing but a man dressed in peach, Eastern clothes walking down the sidewalk with the high school in the background.
A man, distracted by the beautiful jogger, drives up onto the sidewalk and hits a phone pole. He gets out with his cell phone and checks the damage. The stranger sees the incident and smiles.

'I guess some things never change.' He thought.

The End . . . Or is it?

Here's your own Personal Journal to get you started :)   ~Uncle Billy

DREAM JOURNAL

Time :   **Day:**   **Date:**

Dream Topic:

Dream:

DREAM JOURNAL

Time :   **Day:**   **Date:**

Dream Topic:

Dream:

DREAM JOURNAL

Time :   **Day:**   **Date:**

Dream Topic:

Dream:

DREAM JOURNAL

Time :   **Day:**   **Date:**

Dream Topic:

Dream:

DREAM JOURNAL

Time :　　　　　**Day:**　　　　　**Date:**

Dream Topic:

Dream:

DREAM JOURNAL

Time :　　　　　**Day:**　　　　　　　**Date:**

Dream Topic:

Dream:

DREAM JOURNAL

Time :   **Day:**   **Date:**

Dream Topic:

Dream:

Afterwards:

Thank you for purchasing this book… It is the culmination of years and years of hard work and creative inspiration in the midst of giving up altogether - we hope you enjoyed the read and look forward to the next publication which is coming soon…

~ Uncle Billy